THE MAGUS'S HOUSE

ARCANA

Charity's Story

More Coming Soon!

THE MAGUS'S HOUSE

HOUSE

For Terry —

H. T. Brady

This is a work of fiction. All of the characters, organizations, and events portrayed in this novella are products of the author's imagination or used fictitiously.

Published by H. T. Brady
www.arcananovels.com
ISBN: 978-1-7324001-1-5
First Edition: August 2018

Cover Illustration and Design by
Kaija Saaremäel and Silver Saaremäel

For Silver and Kaija.
It took every polar bear.
And I know you would have sent more
if I needed them.

Prologue

Have you ever felt like everyone else knew what was going to happen? It came as a complete surprise to you—but everyone else saw it? And now, looking back, it seems obvious?

That's how I felt about being back in the City and about walking the Fool's Path. Everyone else seemed to know I would be staying. No one—from Delia to the King of Wands—was surprised when I made the choice to walk the Path which would make me a member of the Court of Wands, if I survived.

A small part of me appreciated the irony of my decision.

Most of me was just blindsided.

None of me would have made that choice if I'd known that my mother, the Queen of Wands, was still alive.

I only came back to the City when I believed she was dead. Now here I was, committed to the Fool's Path, and it turned out that her death was an elaborate trick, a part of her incessant scheming.

I spent the early days of her return recovering from the battle which accompanied it—I'd almost died. Again.

As soon as I regained my strength, my mother started sending notes to invite me to lunch or tea or to take a walk. I ignored them. Instead of taking the hint, her messengers became more insistent. So, I began to avoid the invitations all together by exploring with Delia. Together we went poking around the Palace of Wands.

Once, she and I came around a corner—giggling, like we were kids playing a game of hide and seek—and found ourselves facing a door carved like an owl. The eyes were enormous chunks of amber, the feathers picked out in detail from the warm polished wood, and the talons cast in tarnished copper. One hooked claw protruded from the door, forming a handle.

Suddenly silent, we pulled open the door and found ourselves standing in a small ballroom. Sunlight lanced down from skylights shaped like owls in flight, glittering on the mosaics on the walls. We left footprints in the dust and did not speak. When we'd had our fill of this forgotten room, we left and closed the door again.

I didn't realize it, growing up, but I've always seen my mother's version of the City.

She *hates* the City.

I thought she had reason to fear it and to make me afraid. And she did. But that wasn't the whole story. Fear never is.

This place is dangerous, but it's beautiful too. It has cozy shops and gorgeous boulevards next to the perilous alleyways and lonesome mausoleums. Almost always *right* next to them.

That abandoned ballroom is as much a part of the City as my mother's mind games.

I have to remember that.

My war with my mother is a battle on many fronts— but remembering that it's her who hates the City, and that I don't have to, is perhaps the most important.

ONE

Amateur Renovations

DELIA SAT ON MY BED WITH ALPHONSO in her lap. The fluffy black cat was half-asleep, purring with his eyes gone down to yellow slits. I stood away from them, facing the blank wall of my room with my tarot deck in hand.

"I'm not so sure about this," I said for the umpteenth time.

"Come on!" said Delia, queen of enabling. "I want to see how this works. It's not really a wall, right? The fabric of this world is different and all that? Plus, I don't want to have to change out of my pajamas every time I come see you. Alphonso needs the extra space to run around too."

Alphonso's ears pricked up at his name and I hid a smile.

"You just want him to wake me up too."

Delia had been given a set of rooms very similar to mine and right next door—she'd regretted that there

4

wasn't a direct door linking the rooms together. I'd made the mistake of telling her that we could fix that—that in the City our physical surroundings were more pliable than they seemed.

Naturally, she wanted to see a demonstration. And a door.

People who were professionals at manipulating those surroundings—at creating the whimsical and intimidating structures of the City are called builders. That's what my father did, before my mother let the Swords kill him.

I, however, had never performed this kind of magic. I was getting cold feet.

"You're supposed to be practicing with your deck, right? This counts, doesn't it?" asked Delia.

"I guess."

"Then I'm being helpful," she said, with a bright smile.

I laughed and put a hand to my deck. She was right, I should practice. I'd been avoiding this. Living tarot decks—those used by the Minor Arcana and their favored retainers—change to reflect their owners and the shifts in the Arcana themselves. They have opinions when you leave them in a dusty box for seven years.

In my defense, I'd been tired.

I'd successfully dodged my mother's increasingly passive aggressive invitations, her servants more and more distressed with each refusal. Yesterday the invitations stopped. I'd thought that either she'd decided to take a day or two off from badgering me, or that she was about to send guards to haul my ass out to see her. I was wrong. She didn't do anything so obvious or straightforward.

She'd sent nightmares. I spent the night tossing and

turning, going from one horrible dream about her to another. I'd woken exhausted and grim this morning, trying to figure out what to do to counter my mother's latest gambit.

"So what card do you use? Does it have to be a Wand?" asked Delia.

The palace—yes, palace—in which Delia and I currently resided belonged to the Court of Wands. "Wands" as in one of the four suits of the Minor Arcana of the tarot.

"No. I can use Swords or Cups or Disks too," I said, naming the other suits of the Minor Arcana. "Technically, I could use the Fool now, or risk the wrath of the other Major Arcana by using their cards without their countenance. That tends to have significant unintended consequences though—not least of which is attracting their attention. I'll have the easiest time with Wands—they'll be the most sympathetic to doing what I want." Because we stood in the Palace of Wands, and because I'd been an initiate of that Suit since I was a child—able to wield fire through magic—and because my mother was the Queen of Wands.

"I see," said Delia, with a 'go on' look on her face. Delia was my roommate and best friend from the mundane world, and ever since she'd seen the City—with its living tarot cards, its magic and weirdness—she'd been fascinated. It helped to see this place through her eyes— without my family baggage. It was weird too.

"Okay..." I focused on the wall. I ran my finger along the tops of the cards, searching for the one that felt right. I shouldn't have to dig through my deck to find the right card for a job—it should jump into my hand.

My deck seemed sluggish. Annoyed. I focused harder on the idea of a doorway. I needed a door in the wall.

I took in a deep breath and pulled a card.

It was the ten of wands.

My ten depicted a woman with severe black hair pulled tightly away from her face. Loaded on her back were a pile of sticks—the ten wands. It's a card for carrying burdens, great burdens that are nearly too much to handle.

My mother was disguised as the Ten of Wands before she revealed herself. I'd found out later that the real Ten had helped her—assisting from faraway with the spell that kept my mother concealed.

The ten of wands was not a helpful card for making a door—there was no change in it, no threshold, only perseverance. I tried to see the angle, the meaning that would let me use the ten of wands to do what I wanted to do. I failed, sighed, and put the card back.

"What happened?" asked Delia. "Did it not work?"

"My deck is annoyed with me," I said. "I may have to search through for the right card."

"Your deck... decks can be annoyed with you? They have personalities? Does it talk to you? Like a cursed sword or something?"

"Living decks, like mine, can be annoyed, they sort of have personalities, it doesn't talk to me and no—not like a cursed sword or something." I'd gotten good at following all of Delia's rapid fire questions.

I focused again on making a door and on feeling contrite towards my deck.

"You could just burn a door in," suggested Delia.

I laughed. "Great plan."

Each of the four elements correspond to different suits in the tarot. We Wands use fire. Accidentally, I'd tied my fire magic to my temper. Getting angry meant I set things on fire. Something I should learn *not* to do.

I pulled another card, hoping that my cards would work with me.

I drew the two of disks.

The two of disks is a balance, a shifting between one and the other—opposites held in contemplation by a central figure. Disks—being aligned with earth—usually have to do with the physical world. My card showed a young man with a wide smile, holding out one disk to each side. It might have been a precarious pose, but it was clear that he knew what he was doing—was perfectly balanced and would not let the disks fall.

The two of disks would do quite nicely.

I focused on the card and the idea that a wall and a door are opposites. I held up the card so that I could see it and the wall I wanted to make into a door. I thought about what it would look like, how nice it would be for Alphonso to be able to wake up both Delia and I. I thought about staying in my pajamas and about doors.

At first I thought nothing was going to happen, which annoyed me. Although it shouldn't have—it wasn't like I'd had a lot of practice with the cards. I'd mostly set things on fire...

That was the wrong direction to let my mind stray. My irritation and the thought combined with my concentration on the door and the card, suddenly amping up the spell. A burst of power ran through me and the card—struggling to harmonize since disks and fire don't go together.

Part of the wall exploded in a puff of plaster and dust and splinters. Delia let out a shout, Alphonso shot under my bed, and I sat down hard—not used to that much power running through me. Having drawn in a full breath of dust, I started coughing. My outer door opened up, and my servant Rosette appeared, alarmed.

"Miss Waits? Are you well? Hello?" she said and then started to cough herself.

"We're fine," I coughed.

Alphonso yowled his disagreement.

The dust cleared somewhat to reveal a rough doorway-shaped hole in the wall between Delia's room and mine. It was a little jagged, the edges somewhat singed, but upon further inspection it did have a lintel and some little resemblance to a properly constructed doorway. Not quite a resounding failure. Just close.

Delia, covered in dust, peered at it critically for a moment and then she grinned at me.

"You made a door!"

"Sort of," I said.

"You're a wizard, chérie!" she said in a gravely voice.

I laughed and shook my head.

Rosette was staring at the mess, and I felt suddenly bad. "We'll clean it up," I said. "Sorry for the excitement."

"Oh, no trouble at all," she said—in the same voice I used to use when I was super annoyed and couldn't show it. "You need to get yourselves cleaned up anyway," continued Rosette, with a sigh.

"Why?" I asked.

"The Wands Conclave. It's almost time."

"Ah," I said. The entire House of Wands were summoned together to see their Court reunited. Mostly. I'd tried to get out of it—but the King had insisted I be there, since I was on the Fool's Path now. Ordinarily, I would have argued with him, but he'd seemed so tired when he asked that I acquiesced with 'nearly-good-grace'—as he'd put it.

"We'd better get ready then," I said.

TWO

Behind the Thrones

DELIA AND I CHANGED. Rosette made a half-hearted attempt to bully me into a frilly red dress, but I wasn't having it. I wore a red jacket, embroidered in gold with a high collar over a black shell and black pants. I looked a bit like a nutcracker, and I was okay with that. Delia, on the other hand, opted for billowing yellow silk pants and a matching top made of embroidered and beaded panels laced together in the back. *She* looked like she was stepping out of the *Tales of the Arabian Nights*.

When we were ready, Rosette led us into the palace, taking a route I wasn't familiar with. We traversed long hallways, climbed down two narrow back stairs, and crossed a handful of rooms each decorated in disparate styles. Only in the City could you go from baroque sitting room to tatami floored tea room to an art deco stairway and back again in so many rooms.

"Where is this Conclave?" I asked, finally.

"The throne room," said Rosette. "We're nearly there."

She took another turn, with Delia and I following like brightly colored ducklings.

I realized I'd balled hands into fists. My mother would be there. This was the first time I'd be unable to avoid her. I flexed my hands and let out a long breath.

"You okay?" asked Delia.

"Yeah," I lied. I took another breath and tried to let go of my anger, to be cold and collected.

Rosette stopped in front of a narrow door—more like a cupboard than an actual door—and said to me: "Through here and down you'll find the waiting room behind the thrones, miss."

"What about me?" asked Delia.

"We'll go down and through the proper way," said Rosette. "Miss Waits needs to go with the Court."

Delia hesitated, looking at me. I nodded. "It'll be okay," I said.

Delia snorted. "I'll be as close as I can get," she said.

"Thank you," I said—there was more to say, but in the end she already knew it all. Delia winked, of all ridiculous things, and took Rosette's arm. "Alright, let's go see what this throne room is like. Onwards!"

Rosette blushed a charming pink, and I thought Delia might get her to forgive our little renovation project after all.

They disappeared, leaving me alone with that narrow door.

My nightmares from the night before trod into my mind: myself screaming at the bottom of pit—knowing my mother could get me out, and that she would come, if only I begged. Being a child, chased through an empty house by something I couldn't see. There were more. She's creative, my mother.

I glanced around for something convenient to set on fire, but there was nothing to hand. I'd just have to keep my temper.

I squared my shoulders and opened the narrow door.

A short cramped spiral staircase led me to a dimly lit and comfortable sort of living room. A fire crackled in a fancy black marble fireplace and the room was warm. Large overstuffed couches and chairs hugged the walls, but no one was sitting in them.

The Court of Wands awaited me.

The King wore his habitual turtleneck and slacks, with a gold robe over them. He wore his narrow crown and stood with his eyes closed, head bowed and arms folded in a corner away from the Queen.

The Queen of Wands, my mother, dressed more traditionally for her card: her golden hair piled on her head into a crown of braids, her gown made of overlapping silk ruffles in shades of red and orange. Behind her stood the severe Ten—the only numbered card in the room.

When I stepped off the staircase, my mother sent a dazzling smile in my direction. I'm sure anyone else would have found it charming. I gritted my teeth in a smile of my own, and then turned sharply away feeling sick. I hated that my heart sped up around her, that I was filled with jittery energy and my stomach twisted into a knot of anxiety. I hated that she could have that effect with nothing more than proximity and a fucking smile.

I tried to ignore those feelings and went to stand by the Knight of Wands. I was grateful for the fire in the fireplace and fed little bits of my anger to it as carefully as I could. It huffed and roared and subsided as I spent my magic.

The Knight was paler than usual, his arm held across his chest in a white silk sling. He wore one of the three piece suits he favored, but he didn't seem quite like himself. I hadn't seen him since I left the infirmary.

"How are you, Sir?" I asked. I kept my voice down—it seemed appropriate for the setting.

He turned to me while keeping his eyes downcast, their blue shadowed.

"I'm well, thank you, Miss Waits."

"*Miss Waits*?" I asked.

He corrected himself: "Charity."

"Well is pretty good, considering where you were a few days ago."

"Stabbed?"

"Stabbed."

He'd been run through by the Knight of Swords less than a week ago. I was surprised to see him on his feet— and not surprised to see that he really didn't look like he should be.

My concern must have shown, because he managed a wan smile.

"I'll go right back to bed after this," he said, in answer to a question I'd resisted asking.

"Good," I said. "What is all this, exactly?"

"We're addressing the House—every Wand. They know that Her Majesty is back, but there's some confusion about—" he stopped himself. I saw his eyes flicker towards the Queen, but he didn't actually turn. She was speaking to the Ten, their voices as low as ours.

"Have you spoken with her?" he whispered, even quieter.

"No," I said, and then continued before he could express an opinion about that: "So what am I supposed to do? I don't have a throne or anything. I'm not the Princess of Wands." *Yet.*

"You'll sit below the throne," he said. "On the stairs. The throne furthest to the left as we enter."

I nodded and gulped.

"What? You don't like being on display?" the Knight asked, and it took me a second to realize he was teasing me. He already knew that.

"Wands?" My mother's voice called us to attention. I jerked when I heard it—the sound of her was enough to set me on edge. I stepped back, putting the Knight of Wands a little between us and then feeling bad for doing it—his relationship with my mother wasn't exactly uncomplicated.

The King shook off his weariness and crossed the room to offer his arm to my mother. She took it. The air shivered around them, as they summoned up the auras of their cards—and for a moment I saw the King dressed in rustling cloth of gold, a more elaborate crown on his head and a lion at his side. My mother's gown danced like real fire, her hands heavy with red jewels in gold settings. She was tall, her face bright enough to burn an afterimage onto the insides of my eyelids.

I don't think I gasped, but I might have. World damn her.

"Charity?" asked the Knight.

He offered his good arm to me.

"Right," I said. I put my arm through his, and glanced up at him. I caught a glimpse of a golden helm with a white plume, a cloak of rippling red velvet hung from the back of his shoulders, the fabric embroidered in gold with wands. Then he was my familiar Knight of Wands again.

"Ready?" he asked, as the Ten of Wands opened up the door for the King and Queen. With the door open, I could hear the noise in the throne room—the chattering of hundreds of people abruptly audible.

As the King and Queen stepped out and appeared before the crowd, the noise rose to a greater pitch. The House of Wands cheered their King and Queen.

"World damn," I said, and the Knight looked amused as he pulled me with him into the room.

THREE

Full House

THE THRONE ROOM OF THE Palace of Wands is tiled in red and black and orange. Great pillars of stone support a roof decorated in golden flames and suns. The pillars are shaped like burning brands and each has a brazier beside it—with fire leaping and dancing in different colors throughout the room. It's a space that, like a cathedral, cries for you to look up into the darkness of the ceiling and find the divine in the shadows.

Four thrones on a raised platform dominate the room—each carved from single chunks of pink veined marble and decorated in gold.

The door we used was behind the thrones and below the platform, hidden from most of the room. The Knight and I climbed the few steps up to the level of the thrones and as the King and the Queen parted to take their places I could see the crowd.

The numbered cards, the retainers and servants, and the guards of the House were all there, filling the space between the pillars. Some climbed on the plinths of the braziers to get a better view of us. I'd never been in front of so many people in my life. I shook—buzzing with unspent and useless energy that told me to run away and hide. As I watched, a few bursts of fire lit up over the heads of the crowd—like miniature fireworks.

Fuck.

I knew I was on the Fool's Path, but I may not have thought it through entirely.

The Knight walked us to the front of the throne's dais, then gently pushed me to the left. I tore my eyes from the howling crowd and went to stand in front of the throne on the far left. I was relieved to find myself next to the King of Wands and not the Queen.

When we were all in place, the King sat—then the Queen and then the Knight. I almost forgot to sit on the step instead of the the throne itself and only remembered at the last minute. Thank the World I'd gone with pants and not a frilly skirt.

That thought reminded me of Delia, and I searched the crowd for her.

I found her close to the front and center, the Seven of Wands beside her. She met my eyes and smiled, nodding encouragingly.

I swallowed and tried to smile back, but I don't think I did it right. She didn't seem particularly reassured.

As the cheering and yelling subsided, the Queen of Wands stood up. This incited another spirited yell from the crowd, before fading away respectfully. They had their Queen back.

I remembered the King of Wands telling me that sometimes a Suit failed entirely—that we could be destroyed and that Wands had appeared to be heading that way. I tried to imagine the relief of going from only having a King and a Knight, to having a resurrected Queen *and* an unexpected candidate for Princess on the Fool's Path. Then again, I didn't have to imagine it. The feeling was right in front of me.

My mother smiled down at her people.

"Wands!" she cried, and they answered her.

I glanced at the King. He sat regally impassive, almost like a statue on his throne.

"Wands! How happy I am! How relieved I am to walk amongst you once more! I missed you!"—laughter and cheering—"The last few days have been most strange! For all of us. But now we are all together, so let me share with you what's been going on."

"As all of you know," she said. "As we all are forced to know—the Court of Swords,"—shouts, angry and derisive—"The Court of Swords will stop at nothing to see our Suit and our House reduced to ashes. I will not lie to you—we were hard pressed. We are. Yet still—again as you all know—I will stop at nothing to see them confounded—to see them stymied and vexed and frustrated in their every endeavor."

The room was silent, listening to her. Believing her. I glanced again to the King, but his expression remained the same. What was going on with him? I closed my mouth, which I'd let fall open.

"Knowing me for their implacable enemy, the Court of Swords chose to target me—to threaten my life again and again. A compliment, from them, really,"—short giggles, uncomfortable laughter—"However it meant that I could not *attack*. Counter, yes, but not attack—I could not bring my full power to bear against them. We are the soul of fire, my friends. We are not meant to bat aside a dozen petty attacks, to be worn down by cease-less irritating gusting. We are meant to strike! To burn, furious and bright!"

The crowd liked that. My mother smiled, benev-olent and just slightly regretful, and said, "So I deceived you."

"To create the opening I needed—an opening to strike at the heart of the Court of Swords, I needed to be dead. They needed to believe that I was beaten and gone."

They didn't, I thought. The Court of Swords never thought she was dead. They were trying to find her. The Knight of Swords thought I *was* her. Still, the King said nothing.

What is she doing?

"And they did give me an opening—but the Wheel turns in strange circles sometimes. Because the opening I was given put my Court and my only daughter in danger."

I'd set my hands on the stairs to either side of myself. My palms began to sweat furiously as all the eyes of the House of Wands fell on me.

The Queen, my mother, turned to me too. Her smile was the perfect blend of pride and regret. I looked back at her, and I wanted to throw up. She was so good at this. I'd forgotten how good at this she was.

"I thought I'd lost her forever," she said softly, as though to herself and not to the crowd, eyes still on me. I thought of the nightmares she'd sent. I thought of the expression on her face when she tried to kill the Princess of Swords a bare week ago. I thought of the Knight of Swords and almost dying while she was still in disguise. I was furious and astonished. I'm sure it showed on my face—but everyone would attribute the expression to being angry at the Swords, not at her.

She drew in a calculated shaky breath. As though over-come by emotion.

"Forgive me," she said. "I seek to destroy our ene-mies—always. Everything I do is for our Suit and our House, for our families and our place in the City. I will not let *anyone* touch our Court! Or my Wands!" She meant them. They all thought she would die for them, and so they would all die for her. They roared and more bursts of fire erupted overhead. My breath came faster.

I focused on my hands, on not setting anything on fire, and tried to breath evenly.

"... As Wands, we rise from our embers. I am returned and rested! A Wand walks the Fool's Path! Our Court will be mighty and whole and stronger than ever. Many con-tests and challenges and changes lie ahead. Rest assured that we all will meet them together. Let feeble winds rise—we will feed on them. The House of Wands burns eternal in *our* City."

They were with her. I stared out over a sea of fierce, yelling, and whistling faces. The applause was deafening. I found Delia again. She seemed worried for me. I was still breathing too quick.

21

I funneled my anger towards the braziers—causing them to flare up. People noticed and they cheered me for it—seeing a vengeful daughter, devoted to her royal mother.

The Queen of Wands turned to the King, and he rose without a word. He stepped down to her and offered his arm once more. I saw the Knight of Wands stand as well. The King and Queen turned and walked back between the thrones towards the room we'd come from. I staggered up and walked to meet the Knight at the center of the dais. I didn't want his arm, but I took it anyway and stalked after the King and Queen.

The Ten was there and closed the door behind us.

I dropped the Knight's arm.

"What the *fuck*?" I said.

FOUR

In Which My Mother and I Have A Discussion

THE TEN STIFFENED, OFFENDED. The King had let go of my of mother as fast as I'd let go of the Knight and didn't look back at me. My mother turned to me with one gently raised eyebrow.

"My dear?" she asked.

"What the *fuck* was that?" I said. "You World's damned liar! You *fucking—*"

"That's enough," said the Ten of Wands, stepping in between my mother and I.

"It is not!" I said. "That was a pack of lies. You didn't reveal yourself to save anyone. You did it to try to kill the Princess of Swords—you left me on my own. And him!" I flung an arm out towards the Knight who looked uncomfortable. "You would have let him die! And you didn't fool the *fucking* Swords with your charade. You fooled the Wands. Why? What the hell were you doing?"

23

"Charity," said the Knight, softly, in a warning voice.

I was not, admittedly, at my best. I'd lost most of my control over my breathing and the small fire in the fireplace roared up the chimney in a column of fire.

"If you'd come to talk to me..." said my mother, all patience still.

I shook my head, violently, "Don't you—"

"... I would have explained everything. Let's go somewhere now so we can—"

"No," I said. "Explain yourself. Do it now, in front of them."

"Charity..." she said, "Surely you know why I did what I did."

"I don't," I said. "I absolutely do not."

"My dear," she said, and I snorted. "How else was I to get you back?"

I couldn't breath. She was lying still. She had to be lying.

The Queen of Wands gently pushed the Ten out of the way. "And how," she said, "Could I explain that to the House? That the only way I knew I could bring my daughter—my only daughter—home, was to fake my own death? That I needed her, because only *my* daughter was strong enough to walk the Fool's Path."

"Liar," I said.

She looked at me, resigned. "I know it will take you time to forgive me," she said. "But I believe you will."

Then she stepped past me to the Knight of Wands.

He was in better shape than I was, standing rigidly

straight with his face expressionless. His good hand trembled though.

"My Knight," she said. "Why have you not come to see me?"

"Forgive me," he said, voice hoarse and quiet. "I've not been well."

"He was fucking stabbed," I said, but neither of them paid me any attention.

"I always thought you were better than him," the Queen said, disappointment edging her words.

It took me a minute to understand. She meant the Knight of Swords. She meant she'd been confident he could beat the Knight of Swords.

The Knight of Wands flinched.

"I'm sorry," he whispered.

I opened my mouth to say something about that—but a hand fell on my shoulder and I looked back to see the Ten of Wands. In the dim room, in her black coat, she seemed like a specter—a creature made to serve my mother. I shrugged her off, furious, and turned to see that the Queen of Wands had laid one hand on the side of the Knight's face. His eyes were wide.

"You'll do it next time," she said.

"Yes, my queen," he said.

I glanced around for the King, wondering why he didn't say anything. He'd vanished—left while I wasn't paying attention. I was sure I would have seen him if he'd gone by the spiral staircase or the door to the throne room, but I was equally sure that he wasn't there anymore. I felt abruptly outnumbered.

"Sir?" I said. "I'm going. Come with me?"

He stared at me, as though from faraway. I wanted it to be sorcery I saw there, but I didn't think so. I was afraid it was something else.

"We aren't done, Charity," said my mother. I wasn't sure if she meant the Knight or myself.

"I'm not speaking to you," I snapped, without looking at her.

"Charity..." she said, all condescending exasperation.

"I'm not," I said, and I stepped around her and, compulsively, put a hand out to the Knight. "Come on," I said. He focused on my hand, and then shook his head slowly.

"I'll stay," he said.

I let my hand fall and went to the stairs as fast as I could. I was running when I hit the upper doorway and didn't stop in the hallway. I jogged down the polished wooden floors, ignoring the Wands I passed.

I thought I took the same path Rosette had used, but found myself in an unfamiliar room—one with a grand staircase. I went up. I thought it more likely that no one would be there. The stairs turned, narrowed, and continued. I kept going up.

Before long I found myself climbing a tight square tower—turning every five paces. I stamped my fear and frustration and anger out on the steps as I ascended. Little gusts of flame burst from my feet as I burned away the puffs of dust that rose with each footfall.

I didn't realize I'd reached the top until fresh chilly air hit my face. It was still winter in the City, and the day was clear and sharp and cold.

I looked up and stepped out onto the top of a bell tower. The space was square, with railings on each side, pillars at the corners held up the roof and the bells. A spectacular view of the City stretched out around me.

I drew in a full breath of crisp air, feeling it settle in my lungs.

I heard someone humming and turned my head towards the sound.

On one of the railings, wearing their habitual billowing yellow shirt and kicking curly-shoed feet over stories of empty space, perched the Fool.

FIVE

A Farewell

THE FIRST CARD OF THE MAJOR ARCANA, the Fool rules beginnings and optimism and innocence. They saved my life and accepted me onto the Fool's Path—while I was on the Path, they were my patron. Though they couldn't interfere with the choices the rest of the Major Arcana made about my acceptability or keep me entirely safe, they were on my side. Somehow, seeing the Fool lessened the panic and rage my mother had stoked up. Or maybe I'd beaten more of it out on the stairs than I'd thought. Regardless, I felt calm approaching the Fool.

I scuffed the floor and moved noisily so that I wouldn't startle them before saying, "Hello, Arcana."

The Fool glanced over and saw me—gentle delight spreading over their face. "Hello, Fool," they said, addressing me and claiming me. "Is your heart back in one piece?"

"Yes," I said. "Thank you." When the Knight of Swords attacked me, it was with his three of swords—which is one of the more literal cards. It usually shows a heart pierced with three swords. It would have killed me, if the Fool hadn't decided to save me.

I peered out over the edge of the bell tower. I breathed in more cold air and the beauty of the sight.

The walls around the Palace of Wands marked our borders like an albino snake. Our personal Midgard serpent. The King's gardens looked like something out of science fiction and the ornate palace beside it seemed to come from a fairy tale.

Far below in the grounds of the Palace, stone and concrete walkways crisscrossed like seams in a quilt—connecting buildings, a lake, the biodomes, a great amphitheater and more. Guards in vibrant orange and yellow uniforms marched along the walls that surrounded us. They were, in truth, the least of what protected the Palace of Wands—there would be ancient magic and cards built into the walls themselves. Still the guards looked very fine.

"Why are you here, Arcana?" I asked.

The Fool didn't turn to me, but they were suddenly sad—their lip pushed out in a pout. They rocked on the ledge, and I had to resist taking hold of their arm and pulling them back from the edge.

"I'm here to say goodbye," said the Fool. "You won't be mine anymore soon. Not only mine, anyway. You're going to the Magus's house."

"Oh," I said. "I am?"

The magic of the Fool is innocence, is beginnings. It didn't suit me—while I don't clash with the Fool, we weren't necessarily the simplest fit either. Still. Here I'd been thinking I was eager to get on with the Fool's Path. Now it felt too fast.

The Fool nodded, solemnly. "Tomorrow. It's time for you to find the Magus's house. Inside you'll find all sorts of things. Blades and cushions, folios and sextants, monsters, foci and other nonsense. He's a bit of collector, between you and me. A hoarder of knowledge, like a dragon. Most of what goes into the house doesn't come out, and there is such a clutter! No open air—but that's his affair."

"Foci? My focus?" I asked. Each court card has a unique token of their suit—a wand, cup, disk or sword— that enhances their abilities with cards. It makes them stronger. I wasn't totally thrilled with the idea—what with my propensity for setting things on fire. I glanced down towards the King's biodomes—the damage I'd done there had been repaired.

The Fool shrugged. "I suppose," they said.

I snuck a glance at them, trying to read their mood. I'd never seen the Fool so melancholy. Their eyes were big with tears.

"I'm going to miss you, Fool," they said to me.

"Me too," I said, reflexively. *Stupid. But true.*

The Fool nodded, still staring out at the City.

Then I said, in a rush: "I'm scared. I don't know if I want—" I thought of the crowd of Wands and their cheers, of my mother and the Knight, of the exhausted King. 'Want' might not be the right word. I didn't know if I *could* do this.

"No one wants to walk my Path," the Fool said, seriously.

"That's not so. There are lots of people that do."

"Well..." said the Fool, drawing out the word and then smiling: "No one sane." The Fool shook their head, swishing their feet over nothing, with the wind whipping at their big belled sleeves. "They *think* that they do. Everyone thinks they want to see the World, everyone thinks they want to meet the Devil or the Lovers. Everyone thinks they want to leave me behind and see the end of the journey. It's always the same. One fool to another, you are wise not to want to walk our Path."

They did look at me then, bringing us almost nose to nose: "Alas, we don't always get to choose."

I smiled weakly. "The last time I saw you," I said, trying to laugh off the shiver that went through me at those words. "You said we *always* get a choice."

"Did I?" they asked. The Fool thought about it for a moment, then nodded as though remembering: "They're both true, you know. At the same time. All the time. Always. It's important to remember both. On the Path and off it, Charity, my Fool. You have all the choices in the World and none at all."

Then they turned back to the sky and laughed, shouting: "One must play the cards you're dealt!"

The sun was sinking towards the horizon, and it grew colder by the minute. I crossed my arms and looked out over the City, companionably, with the Fool, thinking about what they'd said—the cold making our breath into little clouds in front of our faces.

"Thank you," I said, eventually.

The Fool nodded, "You're welcome."

SIX

Two Roads Begun

I WENT BACK DOWN TO THE Palace of Wands and found someone to ask directions. I'd gotten entirely turned around. By the time I found my rooms again it was night. Delia was displeased and told me so: "I thought your mother had poisoned you! Or—I don't know! No one knew where you were! I sent word to the King, kitten. They were going to search for you." She hugged me too, and I knew she was more relieved than angry—and hadn't *really* started to worry yet.

"We'd better let His Majesty know I'm okay," I said. "He seemed odd—and more worn out than usual. I should tell him I'm going out to look for the Magus's house tomorrow."

"You're what?" asked Delia. "Wait, let's send Rosette and then you can tell me about it." We did so, and then Delia plopped down on my bed, staring at me expectantly.

Alphonso yowled and came trotting out too. He jumped up next to her, and suddenly I had an audience.

I paced back and forth, full of nerves from the bizarre day. I told her about the Fool. Then I went further back and told her about the Knight and the Queen.

Delia sighed, but didn't seem entirely surprised either.

"He's a mess," she said, talking about the Knight.

"Yes," I said.

"A very *pretty* mess..." she sighed.

"Don't get too attached, Dee," I said. "He's going to have some lasting damage in a best case scenario. She's a fucking monster."

"Not to worry, chérie," she said. "I'm merely lamenting."

I wasn't so sure about that, but didn't say it. Not yet.

I sat down on the bed next to Delia and said, "I'm not sure how long I'm going to need to be out of the Palace to deal with the Magus and his house," I said.

She nodded. I drew a deep breath.

"Look, I know you can take care of yourself," I said. "But—"

"Watch my non-magic novice ass?" she suggested primly.

I laughed. "Something like that."

"I'm going to start training in magic tomorrow," she said, with a smile.

"What?" I asked, and then: "Really? That's wonderful! How? Who with?" It was a relief and exciting. It put to rest the tiny voice in my mind that wondered if Delia would decide to return to the mundane world someday.

"The Seven," said Delia and I remembered seeing them standing together. "We're going to see if I have any aptitude for it—he said there are a couple different areas of magic to try. Even if I'm not very good, I intend to learn a few tricks—Seven said he'd help me with that too. I'm not going to be as useless as I was when the Swords attacked."

She explained that the Seven had warned her they'd be starting slow, introducing Delia to the deck and trying out some of the most common uses for each card before getting into a few basic martial spells used by the House guards.

I closed my eyes and said, "I don't want you to have to fight."

"Not your choice," said Delia, lightly. "I'm determined to be able to do something next time someone tries to impale you with a card."

"Next time?" I laughed.

"Let's be real, kitten. Someone else'll try it—and I'm going to knock the stuffing out of them when they do."

I didn't like the idea of Delia fighting, but I did like the idea of her being able to defend herself in the City.

"They don't stand a chance," I said with a smile.

"Indeed," she said. She looked at me appraisingly. "We need food and you need sleep," she said.

I groaned. I'd forgotten about the nightmares. My mother was sure to send more tonight.

"What?" asked Delia. I explained about the nightmares and shared my suspicion that our brief conversation probably hadn't helped matters.

"Hmmm..." she said. "Isn't there a card that would help or something?"

"Now that I..." I stopped. She was right.

"You know," I said, with a smile. "I think you're going to be good at this, Dee."

SEVEN

The Princess's House

THE NINE OF CUPS IN MY DECK showed a glittering fountain in a sunny garden. The clear and perfect water from the fountain cascades neatly between scalloped ridges in the fountain's edge into nine silver chalices, filling them with blue and purple fire. It is a card for dreams fulfilled and for a world that is better than we hoped, all at once. It's a card to vanquish nightmares.

After some discussion with Delia, I tried sleeping with it under my pillow and focused on the image while I drifted off. It worked, more or less. My dreams felt like I was in a safe and cozy room while a storm raged outside. I was able to sleep peacefully, if not entirely soundly, and I thought that sleep deprivation alone would not bend me to my mother's will.

Delia and I went down to have our breakfast. The night before Rosette had returned from her errand to the King of Wands with word that: First, he was fine, just tired and hadn't felt up to 'witnessing a Waits ladies' brawl'. I wasn't sure I believed that entirely. Second, if it was time for me to seek the Magus's house, then so be it. He said to be careful.

I felt somewhat let down, like there should have been more fanfare with taking on this step on the Path. Fanfare of a sort arrived in the form of the Ten and the Seven.

They were about as different from one another as possible.

The Ten wore her habitual long black coat, with a flash of red stones embroidered on the cuffs, hem, and collar. Two small lapel pins displayed her ten wands. Her face was thin and she wore her hair bound up in a severe black bun. Her expression said that we were all disappointments to her. Her card, the ten of wands, usually showed a figure bent under the weight of the wands they carry or struggle to hold them all together—it is a card for perseverance and burdens.

The Seven, on the other hand, was tall and broad shouldered, with a wide smile and blonde hair he'd recently shorn short. He wore an open vest and loose red pants. I thought he must be adept at a warming spell to wear that sort of thing—even if we were approaching the end of winter. His wands were tattooed on his arms in gold— three on one and four on the other—and his card typically showed one person standing against many.

"You need to wear something else," the Ten said by way of greeting, nodding to my red jacket.

"Why?" I asked.

"You're going out of the Palace alone. The door to

the Magus's house could be anywhere in the City. You shouldn't mark yourself as a Wand."

I looked at the red coat. I'd grown quite fond of it, to be honest. Irked by the Ten's tone, I almost snapped back that I would wear what I liked, but the Seven smiled and softened the Ten's command by saying, "I think it will be safer."

His province was the security of Wands. He was the captain of our guard, as well as a numbered card.

"Are you coming with me?"

"No, Miss. I've an appointment with Miss Delia."

Beside me, Delia clapped her hands. She wore an empty case at her waist, waiting for a tarot deck. Although she still preferred fancier City garb than I did, her ruffled pale orange and pink skirt didn't drag elegantly along the ground. It was short enough to reveal her dainty and fashionably booted feet. She'd also chosen a turtleneck, which reminded me of the King.

"Good luck!" she chirped, eyes big with excitement. "See you tonight?"

"Yes," I nodded. "And you too."

Delia grinned, and it broke my heart a little. She hugged me briefly and then followed the Seven, who waved his own well wishes before they both disappeared.

Which left me alone with the Ten.

"Why are you here?" I asked.

"I'm to take you to the path you'll use to get in and out of the Palace."

"Why *you* specifically?" I asked. The Ten was my mother's creature—she'd helped perform the magic that it made it seem like my mother was dead and allowed my mother to impersonate her at my party. To say I didn't like her would be an understatement.

She sniffed—the epitome of long-suffering patience. "Because I was asked to."

"By my mother?" I sneered.

"By the King."

My surprise showed.

"You sent word to the *King* of your intentions. Not the Queen."

I didn't say anything else as we went back up to my rooms so I could choose a plain black shirt—a button down, fitted to me, cut like a man's dress shirt—and a long grey coat. We made a funereal pair.

The Ten gestured for me to follow her, and I did—trying not to feel guilty for snapping at her. She had helped my mother, I told myself—and tried to ignore the voice that said she was a numbered card, doing her job. It wasn't like the Knight was managing to say 'no' to my mother either, and I wasn't blaming him—not yet. Not too much, anyway.

"Are you paying attention?" asked the Ten abruptly.

"What?" I asked. I hadn't been.

I glanced around—we'd gone outside the main palace, and we were about to go into a stone building somewhere off to the left of the main gate. Over the door of this building was a large stone face—cold and beautiful and uncaring.

"Yes," I said, trying to make myself apologetic.

She sighed again.

I glanced back along the walkways we'd traversed and hoped I could find this place again and find my way back to my rooms.

The Ten led the way into this new building, and I found myself in something that felt like an abandoned house. It wasn't dusty or even dark—it just felt empty. A scent like old perfume lingered, making it seem like it was only recently empty. The walls were painted with murals, showing fiery angels defeating demons. The faces of the angels and demons alike snarled, twisted with hate. A few doorways led out of the hall and stairs led up. The Ten went right and I followed her into a study—still with those murals wrapping around the walls.

"What is this place?" I asked.

Briefly, I would have sworn there was some wistfulness in her face, but only for half a heartbeat.

"This was the home of the Princess of Wands," she said.

Without elaborating further, she walked to the desk—an elaborate piece of furniture with a dozen tiny drawers, small shelves, and cabinets. She pulled out one of the drawers and set her hand into the carving on one side of the desk, holding it there so I could see the pattern of her fingers. She pressed down. The desk swung out on a hinge, revealing a staircase.

The Ten walked down onto the steps and then waited for me.

I followed and she did something that closed the secret door behind us. Then there was a rush of air and fire as she lit a small brazier in the wall with her magic.

I realized when she did that the walls of the stair and the passage below were made from stacked human skulls. A catacombs.

"Fuck," I whispered, jumping when I saw them, suddenly just fine with never having met the last Princess of Wands. If this was her idea of home, I wasn't sure we'd have gotten along.

"Look here," the Ten said, she showed me the lever which would open the door again and let me out. "Swing the desk closed when you're on the other side, and it will click back into place."

"I've got it," I said and hoped it was true. I tried to appear resolute when she glanced at me, and she seemed mildly less disapproving. Maybe that was her resting face?

"Then let's go," she said. She turned towards the dark, ignoring the skulls. I took a steadying breath and followed her.

EIGHT

Human After All

WE'D BEEN WALKING FOR A few minutes in silence when I finally asked the Ten of Wands, "Why did you help her? My mother? Why didn't you tell anyone?"

"She's the Queen of Wands," said the Ten. "She commanded me not to."

"You wouldn't do it for me—" I said, and then flinched at how arrogant that sounded. "You wouldn't do it for the King. Or the Knight."

The Ten's back was ramrod straight. She could have been a toy soldier or a ballerina with that posture. She lit the ensconced lamps—ornate brass lanterns set between skulls—in the passage as we went and snuffed out the fires behind us too.

"The King or the Knight did not ask me. Neither did you."

"They *wouldn't* ask. Can't you see why she *shouldn't* either?"

I thought that would be it, but eventually she said: "Your friend. Miss Delia."

A chill ran up my spine. "What about her?"

"If she asked you to do a thing, and said it was important. Would you do it?"

"I would—but I trust her not to ask unless it really is important."

It took me another few steps of silence before I realized that that was her answer to me. It was a few steps beyond that that I said, "I'm sorry if I was rude to you."

"It's nothing," said the Ten.

"It's not," I said, annoyance flaring, "I'm sorry." *Could the woman accept a fucking apology?*

The Ten shrugged—by which I mean she lifted one stiff elegant shoulder—as though to say that she couldn't care less.

"You disapprove of me," I said. I knew I shouldn't antagonize her—or myself for that matter—but her stiff and unyielding manner made it hard not to see if I could provoke her.

"No."

"You don't disapprove?"

"Miss Waits," said the Ten. "You misunderstand me. I both approve and disapprove. You may make a fine Princess. It remains to be seen."

I had a strange sense of deja vu, remembering my conversation with the Fool. *Every choice and none at all.*

"What is it you don't approve of?"

Silence again from her, broken only by the flat sound of our boots on the stone and the hungry whoosh as she summoned and dismissed fire to light our way. I realized

42

that the passage had a slight uphill slope, and before long we'd reached its end.

The Ten stopped and stepped to the side so that I could see the door beyond. It was wood, and banded with iron. There was a handle, but no keyhole. She reached into her deck and pulled out two cards, then held them up for me to see: the two of wands and the princess of wands.

"The door is cardlocked," she explained, "These are the keycards for this door."

"Got it," I said. I thought I did.

She pressed the two cards to the place where the keyhole would be and the door clicked open.

"Don't forget," she said. "There's a ward triggered by using the wrong cards."

I nodded, mind already turning to the next step. I needed to find the Magus's house and my focus.

"The Court cannot be divided," said the Ten.

I looked back at her. She was slightly shorter than me, with wrinkles at the points of her tightly drawn mouth.

"What?"

"If the Court of Wands is divided, then the numbered cards must be also," said the Ten. "If the numbered cards are divided, the rest of the House and the Suit will be too. You must not fracture the Court of Wands. It would be disastrous."

My mouth fell open, but I didn't know what to say to that.

She broke eye contact. "Be wary of the Court of Swords, Miss Waits," said the Ten, withdrawing. "Come and go only by this way—unless your situation is dire.

The door to the Magus's house will move. Use your two of wands to find this place, if you don't recognize where you are in the City. Do you understand?"

"I do," I said, thinking of the nightmares my mother sent and about the Ten's comments concerning unity. I wondered if she knew about the nightmares.

"Good luck," she said as she stalked back into the corridor, back to the Palace of Wands and her Queen.

I watched her go, becoming quickly distant—as though the corridor was longer than it seemed and she traversed it more quickly than was natural.

I turned back to the door and it opened when I tried the latch. Before stepping out, I drew a card from my tarot deck. I focused on the Magus while I did so, and my deck gave me the right card.

"Thanks," I whispered to it.

I set the Ten of Wands and my mother and everything as much behind me as I could. I didn't know what to expect from the Magus. My card showed a young man, standing straight with one eyebrow arched and his hand outstretched towards me. He held the four symbols of the four suits in miniature in his palm.

This would be the first time I used a major arcana's card. It was weak magic—to use the Magus's card to find his house—and probably wouldn't have gotten me in trouble even if I wasn't on the Fool's Path. Still. Another milestone.

I focused on his card, thinking about the Magus and then I lifted the latch, and pushed through the door. It locked behind me. I kept the Magus's card in my hand, concealed in the sleeve of my coat and found myself on a wide cobbled street. I was alone. I let my feet start to wander, all the while focusing on the Magus.

The first step was to find his house.

I'd figure out the rest when I got there.

NINE

The Magus

I WALKED FOR A LONG TIME. I got the feeling that the house itself wasn't far—but that something was messing with me. I couldn't tell if it was the Magus himself or my deck getting back at me for all the years of neglect.

I almost found the Magus's house by colliding with the front door.

I turned into a narrow lane, eyes down on the stone street and head focused on the Magus card.

I looked up just in time to find that the lane I'd been following—instead of leading to another road—had suddenly ended in a small metal door. It hadn't been there a moment before.

I gulped. The door was red and painted with a tangle of white lilies.

Etched into the paint—like casual graffiti—were the four signs of the suits, all together in harmony.

The door opened when I pushed it, surprisingly heavy to shift.

I put his card away and stepped across the threshold of the Magus's house, shivering as I did so. Power hung in the air, like the charge before a thunderstorm.

The foyer was a narrow hallway. Pegs ran along one wood paneled wall—the opposite wall was concrete and pockmarked, like a bunker. The floor was a black and white checkerboard. The pegs held all sorts of coats and jackets and scarves.

I took off my jacket and hung it. Then I walked past the rest of the pegs, headed for another small metal door at the end of the hallway.

This door was yellow, and I wondered whether I should be leaving marks on the doors—like Theseus in the maze. I had no Ariadne to give me string. And I didn't have a pen.

So I opened the door and hoped I would remember it was yellow.

I flinched walking into the next room, because it was made of glass. It was like standing in a prism. Light poured in and was captured and reflected back at me. The room was warm and stuffy and roughly circular.

"Hello?" I called. "Arcana?"

"Charity Waits," said the Magus, appearing right in front of me, "Fool."

I jumped, of course. He meant me to and I did.

He wore a long robe cinched around his waist with a broad sash—embroidered with cups, wands, disks, and swords. He was tall, his hair was black streaked with grey and pulled back into a long tail. There was something funny about his eyes, but it was hard to tell what it was from the distance—and I didn't want to get any closer.

He looked nothing like the card in my deck, and still it would have been impossible to mistake him.

"Arcana," I said and bowed from my waist.

When I straightened, he nodded to himself, almost disinterested, as though in that moment he'd seen all that was unique or of note about me.

"Welcome," he said, voice a bass rumble, and I staggered under the weight of the word. It was its own magic, that word. It was him accepting me as his student, and it echoed through the house—giving me a sudden and disorienting sense of the scale of the Magus's house. It wasn't a place in the City—it was a mansion laced through the City itself, entwined with it like a heart whose veins ran under streets, inside the walls and gardens themselves.

The Magus stepped away and began to walk in a slow circle around me, hands clasped behind his back and his slow low voice—for the most part—taking on the timbre of a professor.

"People prepare in many ways for the rigors of the Fool's Path. They study and train and practice. I cannot say you are the least prepared candidate that has ever crossed the threshold of my house — for there have been many and more in the history of the City. You are both uniquely suited to the Path and uniquely unsuited to it. What is it you wish to learn here, Charity Waits?"

I always hated pop quizzes.

"I'm sure you'll tell me what I'm supposed to

learn," I said, flippant. Maybe not the best choice, but I was nervous and sweating buckets standing under that glass dome.

The Magus pursed his lips, not impressed.

"Discipline, perhaps?" he asked. I winced and acknowledged his point with another small bow.

He continued to stare at me critically.

"You've tied your magic to your emotions. To anger, specifically."

"Not on purpose," I said. "I didn't know I was doing it." Not a stellar defense.

"Hmmm..." he said. "You remind me of your mother."

It shouldn't have made me angry. Not the way it did. Unreasonably though, it did. It infuriated me. How dare he compare me to her? Fire leaked out of my fingertips. Try as I might, I couldn't stop it. I was terrified now, but still angry too. The room was already hot and became warmer as I tried to burn off bits of my anger in little flashes. It wasn't working. I was furious and very close to destroying myself.

The Magus's hand moved—like he was brushing away a spiderweb. My anger evaporated, vanishing as quickly as it had come. It was a spell. A fucking spell.

I turned away from him, walking with quick sharp steps and working to get both my breathing and my new, real anger under control.

This I could calm. Sort of.

"Interesting," he said, and he did seem interested. Like I was a new experiment.

I kept focusing on my breathing. I could put off using all the magic pooled inside me from the fury, but I would need to burn it off sooner rather than later. There was nothing in the crystal room to burn.

He watched as I struggled for control and then said, "You will practice control to earn your focus and my countenance while you are in my house—with the purpose of unlearning this barbaric habit of letting anger manage your magic. You cannot rely on your emotions for power, Charity Waits—it puts you and those around you in danger. You have the freedom of the house. You'll find that the house itself is as much a teacher and a test as I am."

I wanted to swear at him and tell him exactly what I thought of the trick he'd just pulled—but I do have a little discipline in me. Or maybe just some self-preservation.

"So... I look around?" I managed to ask. I unclenched my fists.

"Certainly," he said. "For today, anyway."

"Anything I should stay away from?"

The room laughed at me. The Magus's mouth didn't twitch, but the glittering glass walls seemed to bend with hilarity that crackled like breaking china. I got the feeling again of standing at the heart of some great beast, with veins running to the edges of the City. I tried to stay calm with moderate success. If I hadn't already been so filled with rage, I would have been scared shitless by a laughing room.

"The house keeps its secrets," said the Magus. "Everyone enters my house at their own risk."

"I see," I said. I didn't, but I had a feeling that asking more questions wasn't necessarily going to make things clearer for me.

The Magus knew and smiled.

"Good luck, Charity. Show me your mettle and discipline. Your resourcefulness. I would be disappointed if you die."

With that chilling comment, the Magus disappeared.

TEN

Escape the Room

I WAS LEFT ALONE IN THE glass room, the light dimmed without the Magus's presence. I looked behind me for the blue door. It wasn't there.

A part of me expected that. A part of me panicked. I really needed some part of this experience to be slightly normal, for my sanity's sake.

Next I searched for another doorway—or at least a way out of this room. I distinctly didn't want to be here—and I needed to set something on fire. Preferably not myself.

The glass was ribbed and pebbled so that it was hard to see anything beyond—lights and colors and shapes that could have been anything shifted slowly outside the room. I walked around the wall, fingers running along the edge, trying to find something to get purchase on— some catch or ridge or gap that might show me where a door was.

That yielded nothing.

I unbuttoned the top of my shirt and my cuffs—rolling up my sleeves and trying not to let the panicked part of me win out.

I wasn't going to die in the first room of the Magus's house.

I heard someone shout below me.

I looked down. The floor—also glass, also semi-opaque—seemed like one large piece. It was smooth to the touch when I knelt down, trying to see whatever was making the commotion below me.

The yelling continued and the fact that someone else was panicking made it easier for me not to. I ran my hand along the floor. There were no seams, no fault at all in the smooth glass.

"Hello?" I yelled and banged my fist on the glass. That hurt, so I stopped.

The muffled voice below me said something, but I couldn't make it out. I sat back, looking around the glass room again.

Was it getting smaller?

It seemed the Magus wasn't joking when he said I could die here.

I glanced around the room, hoping the door would reappear or that some magic of the house would give me a tool to break the glass, but I was still the only thing in the room. Breaking it with me didn't seem like a great plan.

I didn't have anything to work with. The walls were definitely moving closer, the air thickening and tightening.

At the corner of my mind was a sort of tugging—a

thought that wanted to be heard and that I simply did not have time for. I pushed it away and it pushed back hard.

It was my deck.

I fumbled with the leather and snapped open the case for my cards. One card fairly leapt into my hand—the two of disks: the same card I'd used to make the door with Delia. I pressed it to the floor, focusing violently on shifting to the opposite—to a hole where the floor was.

I fought to narrow my attention to that single point, ignoring the encroaching glass. Like coming down too fast on a teeter totter, I felt the world shift. It slid suddenly in the direction I wanted it to go and I was falling through the floor before I realized it had worked.

It was a drop of about seven feet, broken by a table. I hit the wood with my shoulder and bounced onto the floor—all the wind knocked out of me.

I lay there, trying to understand what had happened and where I was. Slowly, I noticed that the shouting I had heard was somewhere in the room with me.

I was scared to move—afraid I would discover that I was injured when I did. I shifted. My shoulder protested, bruised down to the bone, but not broken. I looked briefly up. There was a glass window in the room—like a crystalline skylight. It was completely intact.

Grateful and wary, I stood up and tucked my two of disks back into my deck while taking in the room.

It was a study or library of some kind. Books lined the walls and glass cases held oddities I didn't have time to explore at the moment.

In one corner there was a man facing off against a... shadow?

It was a spiky shadow, and if I couldn't see the claws and the teeth I knew they were there. From frying pan to fire to shadow monster. I was shaken by my fall and from my interview with the Magus, but apparently now was still not the moment to rest. While I watched, the man stumbled backwards—falling out of my sight behind a desk.

There was a sword to hand. I reached for that.

My hand touched the pommel and it burned the hell out of me. I let out my own yell and snatched my hand away, glaring at the weapon.

Fucking Swords.

That got the attention of the shadow though. It turned towards me and now I could see the thing's teeth. It was the size of a big dog and looked like it had strolled out of the closet of some child's nightmares.

Fuck this.

I put up my hands and released all my pent up anger and fire in as small an area as I could manage. I sent a lance of fiercely hot flames at the heart of the shadow. It screeched when I hit it, the sound freezing my bones. It fell, becoming a twitching heap of matted black fur, spiny claws, and teeth. I dropped my hands, retreating from what I'd done as the scent of burning meat filled the room.

I'd never killed a creature with fire. I hadn't thought about killing this one. I'd tried to hurt people with fire, but it had been self-defense and I'd never actually managed to do it. This creature had seemed insubstantial, magical—not like an animal, like a pet or—

I wretched and abruptly threw up on the ornate carpet.

I stayed on my knees and shuffled away from the vomit

and away from the creature. As I retreated from the various messes I'd made, my hand came down on a piece of paper. It was a tarot card. I picked it up and turned it over.

It was a two of swords.

The man who'd been cornered by the shadow was making his way towards me, looking exhausted and shaken. He wore pale blue and white. If that hadn't been enough to tell me who he served, the cuffs on his jacket were embroidered with swords.

ELEVEN

Well Met?

THE SWORD FOLDED DOWN to sit next to me. I stared at him, my mind blank panic. He didn't seem to notice, he looked like he'd spent longer in the Magus's house than I had.

Finally, I held out the card I'd found.

"Yours?" I asked. My mouth tasted awful.

"Yes," he said. He took the card and laid it on his knee. "Thank you."

His two of swords showed a young man, standing high in the air, balanced on a point of rock. The man was blindfolded and in each hand he held a sword. They were angled across one another, forming an 'X'. I tried not to stare.

What followed might have passed for companionable silence, if I wasn't remembering the death of the last Two of Swords. My mother had killed her with some sort of lightning bolt—it had burnt that Two badly. Her corpse had smelled a lot like the monster I'd killed.

I almost threw up again.

"Are you well?" he asked, sounding genuinely concerned. He was black, with short—nearly shaved—hair and a neat beard and mustache. Probably a few years my senior, he had a serenity about him—as though, for all he was tired, he was used to shadow monsters and women falling through solid ceilings. Of course, he might actually be used to those things. More than me, anyway.

"Yes," I said. "Sorry, I haven't done... Sorry." I took a breath.

"New to the house?" he guessed.

I nodded.

"You get used to it," he said, gesturing vaguely at the house itself. I didn't think he meant killing things. Then he pointed to the card on his knee. "I'm Hector," he said. "The Two of Swords in training. My thanks for your assistance. I'm afraid I'm not consistent with my constructs yet. I have trouble holding my concentration in dangerous situations—so the house is giving me chances to practice." He shrugged ruefully and flashed a smile. He had a nice smile, sudden and bright and unexpected.

"How long have you been training at the Magus's house?" I asked.

"Almost a week," he said. He must have come right after my party. *Oh World.*

"My first day," I said. I reached for another topic, hoping my brain could catch up: "Out of curiosity, how many times have you almost died? So I have an idea of what to expect."

He snorted. "I've been in mortal danger two or three times? In danger of injury... well, I've lost count," he said.

"How's your first day going?"

"First I got a stern talking to, and then I think I was almost crushed in a glass room and then... well, you've seen the rest of it."

"Distressing," he said, sympathetic. "I spent most of the first day walking through hallways with nothing in them. Rather boring, really."

"I'm jealous," I said. And it was true.

He looked at me expectantly. I blinked and he laughed: "What's your name? What brings you to the Magus's house?"

His way of asking those questions reminded me of Delia, which is why I said what I did next. Stupid as it was in some ways.

"Oh," I said, laughing like I hadn't been deliberately avoiding those questions. "I'm Delia. I've been accepted to serve the Magus."

"Oh," he said, impressed. "Congratulations! That's quite the honor. No wonder he's being hard on you."

"No wonder," I chuckled weakly. Then: "I think I'm going to try to get up now."

I stood up, my shoulder protesting, while I thought about all the things I didn't know about the City and the Fool's Path and the Magus and the Court of Swords. I was feeling particularly stupid, even if I'd gotten away with my lie for the moment.

Hector stood up with me. He was taller, and had a hand out—ready if I needed help, but not presuming. He'd pocketed his two of swords.

"Where did that shadow come from?" I asked. "Are we in danger if we stay here?"

"Good thought," he said, scanning the room. "I don't know. I've run into some strange things almost everywhere, even in my own rooms."

"You have rooms here?"

"Oh, yes, while I'm training. You aren't staying with the Magus?"

Oops.

"I wasn't planning on it," I said. I tried to imagine sleeping here and immediately felt sick again. I ignored the creature I'd immolated. "I'll stay with my family still. Until my training is done. Especially if he's being hard on me." I had no idea how believable any of that was, but I sure as hell wasn't going to be living here.

"I've found that if I keep moving, it seems safer," said Hector. He flashed his smile again. "To a certain degree, anyway. We could explore together? Unless your work needs you to be alone?" He seemed hopeful, and that suited me just fine, since my mission for the day was to look around, try to find my focus, and not lose my temper. Except, of course, our Suits were at war, my mother had killed his predecessor. He'd probably kill me and be rewarded for it, if he knew who I was.

What could possibly go wrong?

Still... I didn't want to be in the Magus's house alone.

"Sure," I said.

"Oh good," he said, relieved. "I can practice fighting with constructs if we need to. Good. Which way shall we go?"

TWELVE

Construct Practice

HECTOR AND I EXPLORED THE Magus's house together. It was nice to have company and for better or worse I found that I liked him. I was pretty sure that would end up being 'for worse' someday. I tried to keep the conversation focused on the house around us and on him.

He'd grown up in the House of Swords, and so far as he knew he'd never had anyone in his family become a member of the Minor Arcana. His parents were proud of him—even though the violent way the last Two died made them worry. It sounded rather idyllic compared to my own experiences.

"How did he die?" I asked, deliberately misgendering the previous Two.

"She," he corrected me. "She died saving our Princess." His mouth twitched, and he said: "The Queen of Wands doesn't care about using Major Arcana, it seems."

"What?" The question came out involuntarily, and then I hoped that I didn't seem too interested.

"She used the Tower," said Hector, something like disbelief in his voice. "To try to kill the Princess of Swords."

"Oh," I said.

Oh.

Shit.

Technically, anyone can use a Major Arcana card for their magic. It's a matter of risk. Walking the Fool's Path earns one the countenance—the right—to use those cards with some safety, but even then, using one of their cards makes that Major Arcana *present*. It gives them a say. It's almost more like praying with magic. Or like gambling with magic. The Arcana can be capricious deities when they feel like it. The Tower was especially volatile and dangerous—representing a swift and inevitable cataclysm.

I hadn't seen the card my mother used when she struck down the Two of Swords with lightning. I'd thought it was the ace of wands or something like that. Apparently not.

This train of thought was interrupted when Hector and I found ourselves in a small courtyard garden, where the lilac bushes reached out and tried to snag our clothes. We picked the fabric out of clutching branches and moved on to another room. Part of my mind was getting used to the supreme strangeness of the Magus's house. Part of me still rejected it.

After surviving the aggressive lilacs, we reached a wide concert hall—filled with music with no source in sight. The sounds of invisible violins, cellos, and a flute hovered in the air. As I turned, searching for the musicians, the sounds changed—moving as though the ensemble were always standing right behind me.

A suit of ornate armor approached us. Hector and I both reached for our cards warily. The suit of armor stopped well in front of us and bowed before drawing a sword. It stood at the ready, waiting for one of us.

"Oh!" said Hector. "I can do this. Hold on, Delia." I started when he called me that and fought down a smile.

He used the card he'd recovered earlier and set about calling up an air construct.

I'd only ever seen an air construct up close when it was trying to kill me, and then I didn't see them summoned—only after they'd been called into being. Wind whipped out from Hector's fingers, wrapping itself around his hand and the card he held. I had a brief and awful memory of being held inside one of the air constructs—suffocating as it pulled the air away from me. Then Hector released the card to be carried by the air he'd called forth. I was surprised to see that it was something like a bird—it had wings, anyway, and the card that was its heart bounced up and down with the gentle swell and fall of a hovering avian.

It was smaller than I'd expected, but it dived at the suit of armor with ferocity—wings slicing and rough claws extended. It caught the armor's swinging sword, threw it aside, and rose unharmed.

I tried to watch both the duel and Hector at the same time. He didn't blink as he stared at his construct, furiously concentrating, with sweat standing out on his forehead. Sometimes his hand moved like the bird's claws—riffling the air a half second before the creature moved.

Meanwhile the air hawk sliced and dove. It used a strange combination of natural bird-like movement and spasmodic shifts in direction. It was magical, after all.

I missed the end of the fight, because I'd turned back to watching Hector. His construct caught the helmet of the armor and tore it off—sending it bouncing across the wood floor. The armor put up its sword and bowed, ending the contest.

Hector raised his arms and then slowly lowered them—the air construct dissipated, little eddies of air spinning away and vanishing. Hector snapped out his hand, reaching out to catch the card. The card flipped away from him. He snatched at it twice, but a trick of the air current carried it away and left it at my feet. I picked it up.

He grinned at me, and then he went off to where the armor's helmet had fallen. Hector helped the armor get the helmet back on straight. Then they bowed to each other again and the armor retreated to a wall and its place on a plinth. The music still swelled from somewhere behind me, filling the room. When Hector was done, I returned his card for a second time.

"Whew," he said, holding it up in something like triumph.

"That was..." I almost tried to avoid being hyperbolic, but sometimes it's not worth it. "That was fucking cool."

He raised his eyebrows at the language and then let out a quick laugh. He wiped sweat from his forehead. "Well, thank you, Delia," he said. "It's much easier when the opponent is willing to fight the construct and doesn't come after me directly."

Something had occurred to me, watching him, and I tried to frame the question casually.

"Working with constructs is difficult?" I asked.

He nodded, "Yes, it's quite tricky work—but I'm particularly bad at it too. My Knight despairs of me." He smiled slightly, affectionately, like he and the Knight were friends.

It was his Knight I'd been thinking of—the Knight of Swords had sent multiple constructs after me in the mundane world. Huge, well-defined constructs. I remembered my King saying that it was harder to work magic—all magic—in the mundane world.

Was that normal strength for a member of a Court? Or was the Knight particularly strong?

"What is it?" asked Hector. "You look ill again."

"It's nothing," I said.

"Won't you do constructs for the Magus?"

"I... I don't know," I said. "I haven't gotten to them yet."

For a moment I feared my ruse was done for, but he shrugged and put his card away.

On a whim, I reached for my own deck. I asked my deck for my two of swords. My deck, however, clearly felt it had been more than enough use to me for the moment. Embarrassed, I shuffled through and found the card.

It was different, of course. Mine showed a woman, standing on a railing, with two knives crossed behind her back. She had long brown hair, reminiscent of the woman my mother had killed. Like all the twos, it was about balance and duality—the two of swords might mean thinking through a choice or walking the line between two choices.

I stared at the card and Hector came to stand next to me. I heard him grunt in surprise when he did.

"A living deck," he said. "It's beautiful. Who painted it?"

"I don't know," I said. "My mother gave it to me."

His eyebrows shot up. "Quite the gift."

"Yes," I said. I hadn't thought about that either.

I put the card away.

"Shall we?" I asked.

We began to walk down the empty-but-still-music-filled hall, the helmet on the armor turning to watch us. At the far end were two doors—identically carved to show blooming lilies. When we reached them, Hector gestured that I should choose which way we went. I shrugged, but he insisted.

"It might be time for you to choose," he said. "I think I have accidentally caused you to avoid your own training today."

I sighed and picked a door at random. It turned out that it was blue on the other side.

We were in the entrance way to the Magus's house, my coat waiting for me.

"There's a sign that it's time for me to go home," I said.

Hector didn't step into the hall—he was staying in the house after all.

"I hope we meet again," he said. "In the Magus's house or out of it." He offered me his hand.

"Me too," I said. We shook hands—his grip was solid and warm—and I found that I meant it.

THIRTEEN

Keep It Burning

W ALKING THROUGH THE STREETS of the City felt simple and safe after the corridors of the Magus's house. I strolled towards the secret entrance to the Palace of Wands, taking in the City at sunset and using the two of wands to guide my steps. It was still cold enough that everyone wore large coats and capes—some people wore swirling yards of rainbow fabrics and others wore simple, straight cut cloaks, or bulky layers of sweaters. I crossed from cobbled to dirt to paved streets and watched the shadows lengthen over them all.

When I reached the entrance, I fished out my princess of wands—with a little hesitation from my deck—and then used it with the two of wands to open the door as the Ten had shown me. Once safely inside, I had a new problem.

The passageway stretched long and dark before me.

This morning the Ten had lit and extinguished lamps to light the way.

I felt around in the dark, finding the two sides of the corridor with my finger tips.

Technically, I could walk in the pitch darkness. The floor was smooth and the way was straight. I couldn't remember anything that should give me trouble—no corridors diverged from this one, threatening to make me lost. Still, walking blind through a dark corridor made of skulls sounded appalling.

I swallowed. To light the lamps, I needed to be angry.

Or I needed to practice divorcing my anger from my fire magic, as the Magus had so strongly suggested.

I took a breath, thinking. Using fire came instinctually to me, and trying to parse what exactly I did without the emotion leading me there was difficult.

To start, I tried to imagine a fire in my heart. A bright happy light that danced and glittered. It was a pleasant thought. I tried to bring the fire into the world and then gagged. It felt like trying to breathe underwater, like bending a finger in the wrong direction. It felt like I was using the wrong path, trying something that was unnatural.

Irritated, I closed my eyes—it was no different from the dark around me. I tried again and failed again. Maybe happiness was too far from anger.

Next I tried sadness. I imagined the flame in my heart as a flickering light alone in the dark—isolated and small.

When I had that strongly in my mind, I tried to pull it out of me.

The gut-wrenching wrongness was still there, like I'd

hit a wall right at my chest. It hurt to try to use fire this way. I let go of the sadness, slapped my palm against the wall, and let out a cry of frustration that echoed down the corridor in front of me.

I lit the nearest lamp reflexively with my anger. Light flared and I could see again. The corridor was as I remembered it, the shadowed eyes of the skulls judging me.

The lights were fixed in the wall—I couldn't take it with me and I was more tired than angry again.

I'd have to figure something out when I got to the other end of the passage so I could open the desk, but I didn't have the strength, anger, or patience to figure this out right now.

Flinching, I let my fingers slide along the walls and started off with my only light fading behind me.

The passage was longer than I remembered. By the time I reached the other end I had enough irritation built up to light the little ensconced lantern there so I could open the entrance.

Coming out of the dark I found myself back in the old Princess of Wands' house. I still didn't like the murals there and hurried out.

I left with a quick step and made my way back to my rooms, looking forward to a bath and dinner and hearing how Delia's first magic lessons had gone.

When I reached the room, I nodded to Rosette and called out to Delia as I opened the door. Alphonso glanced up from where he was napping on my bed, but Delia wasn't there.

I stuck my head back out to speak to Rosette.

"Did Delia come back?" I asked.

Rosette stared nervously down at her feet and alarms clanged in my head.

"She didn't come back," said Rosette. "But the Ten was here asking for her—about half an hour ago."

"What did she want?" I asked. I knew before Rosette answered. Part of me was already running away from her, on my way to find Delia.

"She said the Queen of Wands wanted to speak to Miss Delia."

FOURTEEN

Into the Dragon's Lair

WITHOUT WAITING FOR MORE from Rosette, I sprinted away. I wasn't sure where my mother had her private domain in the Palace, but I knew how to find her. I pulled out my deck and her card came immediately into my hand. I glared at it, willing the card to tell me where she was. Then I set off running.

I'd known she'd try something after the nightmares. I should have thought of this. My exhaustion was pushed aside and I ran with my mother's card in my hand.

My path took me down.

I trotted into another building—it might have been a church in the real world—and found myself pulled to a set of stairs. My mother had set up shop underground. The stairs transformed from ornate baroque decoration to something more akin to a Medieval stone dungeon as I descended. They led me down into a large empty space,

71

more cavernous than a cathedral, with columns marching away in three directions. They seemed to be built of deconstructed and re-stacked greek columns—repurposed and slightly mismatched. Fires burned at the base of every one of them in troughs and cast reflections across the standing water that covered the floor. Walkways wound between columns from the foot of the stairs. I stood there, listening to the fire eating its fuel and the echoes of that sound reverberating through the hungry cavern.

Did I mention my mother was dramatic?

I stepped down onto the walkways and looked around. They curved in several directions and it was hard to tell which would actually lead in the direction the card wanted to go. I set out at a quick trot, choosing the middle walkway—one that took me away from the walls. I hoped it would let me catch a glimpse of where I was supposed to go, even if it didn't lead me there.

After only a few turns I saw a structure before me and, upon approaching, it resolved itself into a cozy cottage—bizarrely out of place in this underground maze. Light shone from the windows and I rapped loudly on the iron bound door using a knocker shaped like a ram's head.

"Enter."

Hearing her voice sent a jolt through me. I shoved the door open.

"Delia?" I called as I did.

It was a one room cottage, a bed with a quilted blanket covering it in one corner and a wood burning stove dominating the other.

Delia wasn't there. The only person in the room beyond was the Queen of Wands.

My mother has hair that can only be described as golden, eyes that are exactly the blue they photoshop into magazines. I'm glad I have my father's looks. I'm sure that always bothered her. She wore a casual robe, belted in gold and her crown was sitting on the foot of the bed.

I was relieved and furious at once. She hadn't gotten Delia alone. She had tricked me.

This wasn't the same as seeing her with the rest of the Court. This was giving in, because she'd figured out how to get to me. I expended what rage I could on the nearby braziers, burning it off.

She pretended to be surprised to see me.

"Charity," she cried and rushed to embrace me. I put out a stiff arm to keep her away, angry that I'd allowed myself to be tricked. I gritted my teeth and nearly stormed out of the room. Nearly.

But I was here. Leaving now wasn't going to mean she'd won any less—and it would tempt her to actually try to get a hold of Delia. I did my best to take the loss with some grace. She'd pursed her lips at my outstretched arm.

"Mother," I said. I put my hand down slowly. She smiled indulgently, and leaned forward to kiss me lightly, possessively, on my cheek.

"I'm so pleased you've come," she said. "Eventually."

Lying. Already. I laughed hollowly.

"Which is strange, you'll admit." I did not admit it. She continued: "Since one would think a daughter would be happy to see her mother restored to life. One would think that a daughter might even want a fresh start, under these circumstances."

"A fresh start?" I said, putting as much acid into my voice as I could muster.

"Charity... let's not begin like that," she said.

"Then how shall we begin? Exactly?"

She continued looking sad and infinitely understanding. She was good at that.

"Charity," she said, "I know you're stubborn. Just like me. I don't want to fight with you. I wanted to tell you how proud I am of you. I wish it could have happened another way, but I can't pretend I'm not happy. Happy as a mother, to see how much you've grown, and as a Queen, to know how strong a Princess my Court will have. I can't tell you how pleased I am that you've stepped on the Fool's Path."

I bit my tongue. She kept going.

"I wish that I could have come up with a way to show you that you belong here. To show you that this City is yours. You'll grow to love it, now that you're staying. I'm so glad this is how it's worked out."

After another moment filled by my stony silence, she said: "I know it will take time. You must forgive me. We've clearly thought of one another differently these past seven years. Won't you sit? You must have questions. We have so much to catch up on." Her hand moved towards a decanter of wine on a nearby table. "Your friend, Delia, for example."

I shivered. "Don't—" I started to say, and then regretted it. I took a breath.

"This is what you wanted to say?" I asked. "This is what you wanted to talk about?"

She seemed surprised, "Yes."

"You wanted to 'catch up'—after you faked your own death to trick me here? After you sent threats and nightmares to coerce me into coming here so we can what— have a glass of wine and I can get over it?"

"If you'd accepted one of my invitations..."

"That doesn't justify this shit!" I yelled at her. My hands were balled into fists. I'd lit the little stove without thinking about it, fire flaring into life. The Queen of Wand's eyes narrowed, and I could see her understanding that I had little to no control. She'd thought I'd been showing off til now, making a point. Now she knew I couldn't control it.

"Charity... this is where you belong. I can help—"

"There must be something else," I said. "There's something you want, some part of this that you're not telling me. Why did you want me back?"

"I can't want my daughter home? I can't want her to have a glorious future in the City by my side?"

"No," I said. "Not you. Why should I be the Princess of Wands? Why do it now, when you've needed a Princess for a year?"

"It was meant to be you," she said, she'd gone colder. I should have noticed and taken it as a warning. I was furious though—and that never makes us smarter.

"Why?" I shouted in her face.

Darkness stirred at the corners of the room. Power gathered around her and one of her own hands was wrapped into an angular fist.

"Because I said so."

She said it the way a bear trap closes, with finality.

In anyone else it might have sounded petulant. *Because*

she said so. From her, from my mother the Queen of Wands, it was the declaration that in the end, whatever she said was what would happen. It was the assertion that whatever she wanted was *what would happen.*

It would have been laughable, if it wasn't true.

FIFTEEN

A Divided Court

MY MOTHER AND I STOOD FACE TO FACE, both of us angry.

"Is that what you wanted?" she said in disgust. "Do you feel better now, Charity?"

It wasn't about feeling better. It was about feeling sane.

"Do I prefer the more honest you to your sugary persona? Well, yes," I said. "Yes, I do. We might as well be clear on why we're both here."

"It's a childish impulse," said my mother. "Only someone who's never been a leader, never had to choose between honesty and success, would think of the truth in that way. Only someone who's never been a parent could think that way."

There wasn't much to say to that.

"Was there anything else, Your Majesty?" I asked.

She recovered herself, there in front of me. Her sneer vanished, the darkness fled the corners of the room, and she was tall and beautiful and sad. Her expression reverted to one of patience—like she didn't deserve what I was doing to her.

"No, my daughter," she said. "You may go. Though I hope to see you again soon."

I didn't say anything—I left her little cabin in the cave and climbed back up to the rest of the Palace of Wands again. On the way I flared every torch or brazier I passed with small fits of my fury.

Once outside I drew in deep breaths and turned my face up to the now dark sky. It wasn't a safe place, I wasn't out of her reach, but it felt better all the same.

The sky over the City is different from the one in the mundane world. The moon is larger and brighter—it seems closer. It waxes and wanes—but even when it's dark it's easy to find in the sky. There are only a handful of stars visible—a scattering of them—and they're bigger and brighter as well. If I survived, I would need to find the Moon and the Star—both Major Arcana—someday. I shivered in the chilly night.

Right now, I needed to find Delia.

She was probably back in our room, worried herself, but I didn't want to waste the time going up there if I was wrong. I'd gotten pretty good at finding people with cards.

Delia didn't have a specific card I could use to search for her, but did I really need that to find her?

I drew a card from my deck, and I think it was feeling sympathetic after my day. It gave me the two of cups. I swallowed. Turns out I was wrong—Delia did have a card.

My two of cups showed Delia and I sitting across from each other at a simple wooden table—each of us had a mug in front of us. Alphonso was curled up under the table, by our feet. I closed my eyes and focused on the image. The direction came easily to me.

I opened my eyes and started walking quickly across the palace grounds.

I turned and went around the main building, passing under the shadow of its ornate wall and many windows. I walked through a darkened formal garden, past skeletal rose bushes and empty flower beds.

A layer of frost covered everything—making it glitter in the moonlight.

I passed a hedgewall and finally saw where I was going. Suspended between three trees was a glorious treehouse. Not a rustic structure, but a polished, modern creation of light and glass and wood. I could see into the lowest level of the house through a large window to where Delia and the Knight were sitting on low cushions, leaning towards each other and talking.

Delia laughed. She was fine.

I almost turned around—to leave them out of it for an evening. I was tired.

I kept walking though, because I also needed to know whether the Knight was a pawn or a willing servant of the Queen of Wands. Delia needed to know that too.

I climbed the stair and opened the door without knocking.

"Chérie!" said Delia, grinning at me. "You made it! How was—"

Then she saw my face, saw that something was wrong.

I kept my eyes on the Knight of Wands. He turned faintly red and avoided my eyes.

"Was it that bad?" asked Delia, glancing from me to the Knight. "What happened in the Magus's house?"

"That's not where I'm coming from," I said, still focused on the Knight.

"Where did you come from?" asked Delia.

I raised an eyebrow at the Knight and he lifted his eyes to meet mine.

"Where was I?" I asked him, searching for the truth there, wondering if I'd be able to tell.

"I don't..." he started, but he was a terrible liar—and embarrassed by trying to lie.

Delia *looked* at him while I let a hiss of breath out between my teeth.

"Your mother wanted to talk to you," the Knight of Wands said. "Is that where you were?"

"Yes."

Delia swiveled her attention to me again.

"When I got back to our room, Rosette said the Ten had been by. Said the Ten was looking for you, Dee, because my mother wanted to see you."

"What?" They both said it together.

The Knight blanched. "Charity, I didn't know she'd— she just asked me to keep Delia from—"

"She *what*?" said Delia.

The Knight looked miserably at her and said, "She wanted a chance to talk to Charity alone, so she asked me to keep you entertained for awhile."

Delia and I both glared at him. I was too tired by now to be pissed and too familiar with my mother's nonsense to be truly surprised. Delia, on the other hand, had plenty of energy.

"You were supposed to *entertain* me?"

"Delia..."

"While my friend—my best friend—was told *I was in danger*—"

"I didn't know about—"

"She thought the Queen had come after me! That was a goddamn threat, having Rosette say that the Queen was looking for me."

"The Queen wouldn't hurt you! She wouldn't do anything to you. She only wanted to talk to her daughter. That's it. If Charity had just gone to talk to her when she came back—"

"That's her line," I said, interrupting him. "And you knew I didn't want to talk to her."

"You don't understand. We need the Court to be united—"

"Quiet, cupcake," said Delia, her arms crossed and her eyes still narrowed at him. "I thought you actually liked me."

The Knight drew in his breath sharply and I felt like I was seeing everything from a distance. I remembered what the Ten had said that morning, about the need for the Court to be united. She was right. She just thought we needed to unite around the wrong person.

"Sir," I said. "You said once that my mother was a good Queen because she takes care of her people. What made you say so?"

The Knight of Wands' face took on a haunted look.

"It was what happened when the Princess of Wands died."

SIXTEEN

The Knight's Tale

IT BECAME QUICKLY CLEAR that this was going to be a long-ish story, so I came properly inside and closed the door to the treehouse behind me. I settled in next to Delia—the seats were cushions, which I thought was odd for the primly dressed Knight of Wands—though here in his house he lost the jacket and wore a bronze colored vest and pants. He'd even unbuttoned the top button of his cream shirt.

"The Princess of Wands that I remember was ancient," I said. Admittedly, I'd only met her on a few occasions and my memories of the City were sketchy—I remembered a big fiery woman, with layers and layers of loose skin. She wore grand hats and couldn't walk anymore.

The Knight nodded. "Yes, she died—it would have been a couple years after you left. She had been ill for

82

awhile. I was on the Fool's Path myself at the time..."
he looked abruptly self-conscious, glancing at us like
maybe he shouldn't be talking about this. We both sat
still and waited for him to continue, eyebrows raised
expectantly.

"I didn't have the chance to know her well," he said.
"She died shortly after I was accepted into the Court.
There weren't as many candidates as usual when I was
chosen to walk the Path. There were fewer to choose from
when the next Princess walked. Even so, it was obviously
going to be Sabine."

He glanced at me expectantly, but I shook my head.
The name didn't ring a bell.

"Who was she?" I asked.

"She—well, she was your mother's protégé."

Delia drew in a sharp breath, but I couldn't muster
jealousy for anyone stuck as my mother's protégé.

"She was good—prodigiously strong. She was young—
which is the only reason I was picked to be the Knight
instead of her. She walked the Fool's Path in record time and
the first thing she did—as soon as she was accepted into the
Court—was to challenge the Knight of Swords to a duel."

I remembered my conversation with Hector earlier that
day and said, "The Knight of Swords. He's prodigiously
strong too, isn't he?"

The Knight of Wands glanced at me. His defeat at the
hands of the other Knight still stung—stoked no doubt by
my mother's disappointment in him. He was ashamed of
losing to the Knight of Swords.

"Yes," he said. "And he's an excellent duelist, even
among the Court Cards."

"Why did she challenge him? This new Princess of Wands?"

"The Queen of Wands and the Knight of Swords have a particular feud. They hate each other. Our Princess wanted to kill him—for her."

"You did too," I said.

He nodded. "Yes, but it's different now. This was before the Knight of Swords swore to kill our Queen. He swore it to Justice. She's not safe while he's alive."

"Oh hell," I said.

"What?" asked Delia.

"You want to be very careful invoking the Major Arcana. Walking the Fool's Path gets you countenance to use those cards, but even so... the Majors tend to take it personally if you don't take the vow seriously. Wait. Is this why we're at war with the Court of Swords? Because the Queen—"

"Let him finish the story," said Delia, hushing me with a waved hand. "Then questions."

I grudgingly closed my mouth.

"The Princess challenged him to a duel. She did it publicly and in such a way that made it difficult for us to talk her down. We tried—the King and I—but Sabine didn't like the King since he opposed her walking the Path. I should have argued more, but the Queen was so sure. She thought that the Princess could do it and so I did too. So did the Princess. She was new to her powers as a Court Card and strong and young."

"They fought and it was close—closer than it had any right to be. She did remarkably well, but..." the Knight breathed out. "He killed her. He ran her through." His hand went involuntarily to where he'd been similarly stabbed.

Delia's hands were at her mouth and, in the silence that followed, I tried not to imagine the new Princess of Wands bleeding out in front of her Court—made complete and then immediately broken again.

"You said this was when you knew that the Queen cared about her people," I said.

He found his way out of the memory and said, "She lost her mind. Her fury. She almost killed them all. She would have, too, except the King stopped her. The King and the new Princess of Swords."

"What happened exactly?"

"It was an official challenge—when our Princess challenged the Knight of Swords—and he made it more so by calling on Justice to witness the combat. And Justice came—the Major Arcana actually sat to witness the duel. When it was over, the Queen of Wands ran to the Princess—and the Princess of Swords went to her Knight and started pulling him away. The Queen of Wands—the sound she made. It broke what was left of our hearts. She summoned a wall of fire and would have burned them all. She would have destroyed half the Court of Swords with one spell—but the King, our King, stepped in."

The Knight, remembering, clenched and unclenched his hands. "He was right, our King. If she'd done that, then who knows what Justice would have done—or allowed Swords to do—but we all wanted revenge. We wanted to vent our fury. We might have too. Except the King of Wands fought the Queen of Wands for control of the fire and in the end, the King won. He's more closely connected to the Ace—and she wasn't expecting him to stand up for the bloody Swords."

"So that was the end of that, in some ways. The Knight of Swords challenged any of us to fight him, but the King told him 'no'. So the Knight swore that the Queen of Wands would die by his hand. Our Queen swore that she would kill the Knight of Swords—but only when he had no Princess."

"Meaning...?" asked Delia.

"She promised to kill the Princess of Swords first, and then the Knight," I said. "Of course, she did."

"You weren't there," snapped the Knight, the old pain new again in his voice. I caught the flicker of his other self—the card he embodied hiding just below the surface—armored in red and gold, sunlight glinting from nowhere on a white plumed helm. "He deserved it. We'd all have sworn."

"Justice was there to hear all that?"

"Yes," said the Knight.

"No wonder the two of them are willing to take their Courts into battle over it," I said.

"Don't make light of it!" said the Knight, angry now. "It was noble. It meant something that she would swear revenge there, in front of everyone, in front of Justice, that she would avenge the Princess."

"The Princess—" I started to say, meaning to point out that she'd issued the challenge in the first place, and then had to stop. I'd put a piece together, but my heart understood what it was before my mind did. My pulse had already sped up when I changed what I was going to say: "The Knight of Swords swore by Justice. What did my mother swear by?"

"The Tower," he said, defiant. "She swore by the Tower."

"That's why she didn't mind using the Tower," I said.

"What?" asked the Knight.

I thought of the lightning that struck down the Two of Swords and of Hector. I didn't want to get into that now, especially not with our Knight.

"What's the Tower?" asked Delia, accidentally saving me.

"Another Major Arcana," I said, "It's for abrupt, unforeseen turns of fortune."

"Sometimes for the better?" asked Delia, always the optimist.

"No," I said. "More like a cataclysmic unavoidable fall."

I was exhausted as I considered the Knight. I wanted him on our side, but I wasn't sure I could get him there tonight. I tried anyway:

"That's when the Suit started to split," I guessed. "When the King stepped in to stop the Queen from scorching all the Swords."

The Knight thought about it for a minute, controlling his temper, and then said, "Yes, I think you could say that."

"The problem is this—and you said it yourself—she was wrong."

He opened his mouth to argue and stopped. His shoulders slumped, and then he sat very still. I kept trying not to imagine the last Princess of Wands dying.

Delia looked over at me, sympathy in her eyes, and we both waited.

"I need to think about this," whispered the Knight. Then he said: "I'm sorry, Charity—about tonight. I didn't think there was harm in it, but I was wrong. I knew you didn't want to talk to her."

I believed him, but didn't say anything.

He stared at his hands. "I need to sleep," he said and got up. Delia and I did the same.

We left him alone, and walked out into the dark together.

SEVENTEEN

Choosing Sides

DELIA AND I MADE IT BACK to our rooms and we let out simultaneous sighs of relief when we got there. I don't know about her, but I was feeling out of my depth. Again.

"I don't believe he did that," said Delia, referring to the Knight. She flopped into a chair and clicked to Alphonso.

"Don't be too hard on him," I said, beginning to pace. "He's going to take awhile to get out of... whatever their relationship was. Is. I think this might have been a good beginning."

Delia snorted, and then saw my face, "You're serious?"

I nodded, "I am, Dee. We need to talk about what I'm going to try to do."

She sat up. "What are you planning, chérie?"

"I'm not entirely sure yet," I said. "But... I'm not going to wait around while she comes up with ways to manipulate and control me. I'll lose that game, and I'm stuck playing—I'm on the Fool's Path—and I won't let her win by default."

Saying it out loud made me feel better already.

"When the Ten was walking me out this morning," I continued, "She said that the Court of Wands needs to be united. The Knight said it too. And they are right about that part. They're wrong that it needs to be united around the Queen of Wands."

"In fact," I said, sure of the words as I said them. "It can't be around her. She'll get us all killed."

"Like the last Princess of Wands," said Delia. I hadn't been thinking of that, but it was a good example.

"There can't be infighting within the Court of Wands—we'll fall as surely as if the Court Cards were picked off one by one from the outside. But I... if I'm going to be the Princess of Wands, I can't do it. I can't be her minion. That puts me with the King—and it splits us. Unless we get the Knight. The three of us together could neutralize her influence over most of the House of Wands. I think. I hope. We'll never get the Ten—but if we can get the Knight. And more numbered cards. It might be enough to keep her in check."

"You're talking very fast," observed Delia.

"I'm nervous," I said, spinning on my heel and continuing to pace. "My mother will realize what we're doing at some point and it'll get ugly. Will you help me?"

"Of course, kitten," she said. "With what?"

"With getting the Court of Wands and the numbered cards back on the side of the King?"

"We weren't doing that anyway?"

"I guess we were, but now—well, now I'm going to counter her deliberately."

Delia smiled. "Intrigue!" she said. "How exciting!"

"Yeah, and dangerous."

"You're mostly asking me to talk the Knight down from his cult-like devotion right? Not fight air monsters or anything yet?"

"Yes," I said. "You'll still want to be careful. I do think my mother cares about him in a way. Like an important piece in a chess game." Delia was in it now. I didn't like it, but weirdly enough my mother using her earlier meant I felt less guilty asking for her help. The illusion that she was safely out was broken and I needed all the help I can get. "Be careful," I repeated.

Delia nodded, seriously. "I'll try. What are you going to do?"

"I need to be able to use my magic without being pissed off," I said. "Or it's going to be used against me. Or us."

I told her about meeting the Magus—about his using a card to create fury in me.

"Oh, kitten," she said. "Okay. Can I help with that at all?"

"I don't think so," I said. "Just learn some magic as fast as you can. I have a feeling I'm going to need backup." I stopped and turned to her. "It was your first magic lessons today! What did you do? How was it?"

Delia grinned and flipped open the little case at her waist—showing me that she had a tarot deck there now.

"Pick a card, any card!" she said, in a showman's voice.

"Ha!" I sat down on the bed across from her chair. Then said, "The Fool."

91

Delia put a hand to the cards. She sat very still, focused on the deck with her eyes down to slits. Alphonso pawed at her and she ignored him.

She drew a card and flipped it up. It was the Fool.

She cackled in delight. "World damn," she said, like a proper City resident. "I only started getting some of them right at the end of the day. Seven said that was good for a beginner."

I laughed too. "I can't do that half the time."

"Well," said Delia, "You're using a living deck that's annoyed with you, chérie. Different all together."

That time I chuckled because it was such a City thing to say—and said in a City sort of way.

"Are you trying to pick up a little of the City accent?" I asked, mock suspicious, as she slid the Fool back into her deck. The accent had been edging into her voice more and more.

She smiled, shyly. "Not super on purpose," she said. "I'm hearing it all the time though. Hard not to."

Delia was fitting in fast.

"So what were you doing today, exactly?"

"Mostly this," she said, indicating the deck. "Trying to learn about the cards and what some of them feel like. I was lucky you picked the Fool just now—easy to remember what they feel like since we've met them. The Seven has started me with the suit of wands. With practice I'll be able to summon fire using the ace of wands' card. He says I can't work with fire until I'm properly initiated into the House of Wands and tied to the literal Ace. Did you know that's where you are drawing your fire from? You never said it that way."

"Vaguely," I said, embarrassed. "I know I'm tied to the Ace of Wands, I guess I didn't think about it that way though—that that's where the fire comes from."

Delia nodded. "The Seven says he'll sponsor my joining the House, if I keep working with the cards and show some progress."

"That's wonderful!" I said. "Congratulations, Dee."

She seemed nearly as pleased as Alphonso, who sat purring in her lap. We lapsed into silence and, having sat down, I felt all the energy go out of me. Fear and anger and magic had worn me out.

"You look like you're about to fall over," Delia said.

Delia got up, taking the now grumbling cat with her. She brought him over to me to say goodnight, and gave me a sideways hug, "Go to bed, chérie. We'll see you in the morning."

EIGHTEEN

My Temper

THE NEXT WEEK PASSED WITH frightening speed. In the mornings, I got up, breakfasted with Delia, and then took my secret passage through the Princess's old house, out of the Palace of Wands, and found my way to the Magus's house. In the evenings, Delia and I exchanged news from our respective days. She'd seen the Knight a few times—he'd come to one of her lessons with the Seven, but hadn't said much. By the end of the week, she managed to use the ace of wands to summon small puffs of flame and delighted in practicing.

Unlike the other numbered cards, no person embodied the aces. The closest *we* had was actually the King. The Ace of Wands was hidden away somewhere in the Palace of Wands, the core of our power and dangerous.

Delia and I agreed that we'd work together when the Seven said she was ready to try the other aces—I hadn't known that even though we were the court of fire, practicing with another ace could give us some control over different elements. Another bit of City knowledge I'd lost or never knew.

My days in the Magus's house took two forms. Some were similar to the first—I wandered the house, avoiding doors that opened on chasms and surviving treacherous gardens and finding my way out of endless libraries. I would have said, before this, that getting trapped in a library might be nice—but to be honest it's the 'trapped' part that's a problem, and the library part doesn't really make it all that much nicer. I ran into Hector occasionally—he'd gotten better at constructs. He summoned birds and larger humanoid creatures when I asked him to demonstrate. He still thought I was training to serve the Magus.

I'd forgotten, that first night, to tell Delia about him. I meant to tell her, but with everything else to keep straight, I seemed to remember at only inconvenient moments—when other Wands were around. Looking back, it's easy to say that I was a tiny bit jealous of Delia's new friendship with the Seven, and the training she was getting—and therefore enjoyed having a secret new friend of my own. At the time, I didn't have the energy to think it through. Yes, yes. It's an excuse. I feel bad about it now.

The second kind of day I had in the Magus's house was when he would meet me when I arrived—he always appeared in a different guise. He would command me to practice summoning fire without being angry. Inevitably the lessons quickly devolved to practicing *not* summoning fire because I *was* angry.

∞

Today the Magus wore his long grey hair tied back in a braid—his embroidered suit was sharp, black, and well tailored. He seemed even taller. His eyes were clear and critical brown. I wouldn't have thought I would miss his more mystical appearance, but that was before I'd met his business-like demeanor.

"Calm yourself," the Magus said to me, voice tense with his own impatience. "Find the reins of your temper and hold them, for World's sake—are you a beast?"

I took a deep breath in and tried to ignore the bastard.

We were in a long concrete room today with dummies standing at one end—as though ready for mundane target practice. I'd already failed to summon magic without anger, *and* set one of the dummies aflame with my temper. I was proud, frankly, that it was only one.

"Ruled by your emotions, you will fall. You need discipline. What have you been doing with your life?"

Finding other ways not to set things on fire. Living in the mundane world where I couldn't summon enormous fire balls.

"If you cannot hold back your anger by will, then draw on something else."

"Like what?" I snapped back.

"Sorrow? Love? Surely you feel something else sometimes, since you feel so much?"

"I've tried that," I said.

"Oh, you've tried it. Once? Twice? All your emotions already?"

I bared my teeth at him and then closed my eyes and took another deep breath. I was angry. Angry at him and angry at myself that I couldn't seem to call up so much as a spark without being pissed off.

I didn't think I could get to happiness or love, at the moment, so I went for feeling sadness.

That was easy—I thought about the last Princess of Wands. I didn't know her—didn't remember her at all. Still I'd become preoccupied by the *idea* of her since the Knight told us the story of how she died. Walking through her house every day didn't help either—though I'd never brought myself to stop and explore. Thinking of her now, I was sad and curious and less angry.

"At least that's something," said the Magus, cold and pitiless.

I kept my eyes closed, focusing on sorrow.

"Now," said the Magus. "Light the dummy on fire."

"Give me a World's damned minute, will you?" I yelled, whiplashing straight back into being angry.

"No!" he cried, furious himself. He threw his head back and directed his next comments to the concrete ceiling, "Why am I cursed with undisciplined Fools? And why is the time so short?"

He came up close to me then, deliberately towering. I stuck out my chin and faced him while he explained again: "The point is to get your magic untangled from your *anger*, Miss Waits. The point is that if you could light something on fire while you felt something other than *anger* it would be progress. Meager progress. Infinitesimal progress. But progress"

"Fuck you," I said, and loosed a poorly controlled burst of magic when I did.

Another of the dummies burst violently into flames.

97

The concussion rushed towards us and threw both of us sideways.

I saw him fall with me. I rolled painfully onto my back, coughing as I tried to get my breath back. I'd hit my shoulder again. I needed to stop doing this. The Magus was already up. He seemed like he'd never fallen at all. He looked down at me, face in shadow with harsh fluorescent light surrounding him like a halo.

"You are unworthy," he said.

I know, I thought, closing my eyes.

The floor was cold and solid. I could feel the rest of the strange house of the Magus beyond it the way I had the first day. It was like a forest, present and vast with sounds and buzzing life. Full of whispers. I listened for a long moment. From here I could almost see the network of magic running through the City—and the presence of the Magus, in the room with me, was like a beating heart. One heart among several. It wasn't really the Magus's house. He was the house. He was part of the fabric that wove together and was the City itself.

"Do it," said the Magus, but I hardly heard him. I was listening to something else and exhausted besides—a burnt out husk. I'd felt like this after blowing up the King's garden.

The blankness was a relief.

The Magus nudged me with the toe of his boot. I didn't want to get up. I wanted him to leave me alone on the floor and let me be. Unfortunately, I knew he wasn't going to. Not until I could set things on fire without being angry. Something clicked over in my brain—like a very innocuous, mundane variety of epiphany.

If I could set something on fire now, he would leave me alone. It didn't need to be big. Just something. Distantly, I thought I heard a door open and close.

The Magus nudged me again.

So I set his pant leg on fire.

There are some things that are impossible until they aren't. We try and try and try and are surprised when, abruptly, it works. I giggled.

The Magus jumped away from me as I opened my eyes. I was rung out, but still chuckling. I'd done it. Set something on fire without using anger. I heard the Magus curse and then laugh too—a deep chocolatey sound. I rolled slowly onto my side and got to all fours and then my knees. That was as much as I cared to do.

Already back to his brisk and business-like facade, the Magus said, "Progress."

The lesson over, he turned his back to me and headed for the door. It opened before he reached it, admitting Hector. The Magus and the Sword bowed to each other, and then the Magus left.

"Infinitesimal," I agreed, though he was already gone.

NINETEEN

Another Farewell

HECTOR SAT DOWN ON THE concrete floor across from me, a bit the worse for wear. One of his sleeves was drenched and he was holding his wrist as though it was hurt.

"Hello," I managed.

"Hello," he said. "Are you alright?"

"Just tired, I think," I said. I giggled, "and bruised." I'd landed on my shoulder again—but nothing that was worse than how tired I was. Practicing magic doesn't seem like it should be bloody exhausting—it's just focusing and sometimes putting a hand out. It doesn't look like running a marathon, but that's what it feels like. I'd been doing it for days now. I was still sleeping with the nine of cups under my pillow—but I went to bed so exhausted that I wasn't honestly sure if my mother was still sending nightmares or not.

"You...?" I asked Hector.

"A flight of stairs transformed while I was on it. It dropped me in a pond." He held up his damp sleeve to demonstrate and flinched. He'd shaved, the lines of his chin and the dome of his head clean and smooth.

"Oh. Your wrist okay?"

"I didn't break anything," he said, chagrined.

"That's good," I said—which pretty much exhausted my capacity for nuance. He seemed like he had something he wanted to say, but he stopped.

The door opened again, the iron weight of it swinging without a sound. Hector and I both jumped, reaching for our decks.

Into the room trundled a low table. It's legs were curved and it's feet bore carved wooden claws, each fastened around a wooden orb. Balanced on the table were a plate of sliced fruit, two large bowls of rice porridge with crispy pieces of chicken on top and a teapot—all with the appropriate settings. It walked with the quick step of a small dog, and didn't jostle its load at all. Behind it came two low, well cushioned stools—trailing like puppies. The table paused just shy of us, becoming entirely still and furniture-like along with its cushion companions.

I turned to Hector, who raised one dark eyebrow.

"He couldn't just fucking say 'well done'," I said.

I'd shocked Hector. He flapped his mouth for a minute and then said: "My. Angry today, Delia?"

"I'm not, actually," I said, picking up one of the bowls and beginning to shovel the food into my mouth. As soon as I started to eat, I knew I was starving. Hector picked up his meal more slowly, favoring his wrist.

He seemed like he was about to say something again.

I waited, but nothing came out. He ate elegant small bites with his spoon and continued silent. As I've said, I didn't have much energy left for nuance.

"What is it, Hector?" I said finally, between chewing.

"I'm leaving tomorrow, I think," he said.

"Oh," I said, then got a hold of myself. "You've finished your training? Congratulations."

"Yes," he said. "This part anyway." He swayed, as though he was walking a tight-rope.

"What's next?" I asked. "For a numbered card?"

"Traditionally, the Two of Swords trains with the Magus, with Justice and with Temperance," he said, naming more Major Arcana. "I'll go back to the Palace of Swords, train with my Court for awhile, and then request that Justice permit me to attend on her."

I remembered the Knight and the Princess of Swords at my party—he'd attacked me and she'd been cold and distant. She'd tried to stop her Knight though, when she realized that I wasn't my mother in disguise. The last Two of Swords had died for her.

I shook my head, reaching for a thought that wouldn't incriminate me in Hector's eyes.

"Well..." I managed. "Let's see a construct then!"

He smiled. He still had a nice smile.

Hector drew a card, one of his twos of swords. He lifted it up and summoned an air construct. It was a spindly thing of wind and bits of dust, small with long twig like fingers. It gave me a little bow, and then Hector let it go. The card fluttered down and he caught it neatly out of the air.

"Wow," I said. "You've gotten better."

Hector tilted his head to the side. He was silent for a long minute, still holding his two of swords.

Hector laid the card down on the table. "You should take this," he said.

"What?" I asked, surprised. "Why?"

He shrugged. "So you can reach me. If you want to. Once I'm done learning in the Magus's house."

Hector took his own overly large bite of the food. I didn't feel guilty, exactly, lying to Hector, but I was sad. I'd never use the card, and if he ever found out why, we wouldn't be friends anymore.

"Thank you," I said, taking it. I put it in the pocket of my jacket, not in with my living deck. "And... how will you find me?" I asked.

"You shouldn't be too hard to find," he said, "you'll be in the the Magus's house. Right, Delia?"

TWENTY

Running the Gauntlet

I STEPPED OUT OF THE MAGUS'S house later that day and onto the street, exhausted. Before me stood an enormous, sand colored building with old looking columns and arches, and a more modern ribbed metal dome on top. It looked like an observatory. People bustled past, carrying packages, holding hands, dressed in every color of the rainbow. Most of them wore little star pins—showing their allegiance to that Major Arcana.

I still wasn't wearing the colors of Wands in public, and while I stood out a little in my monochrome, I wasn't the only person wearing black and grey either.

Joining the throng, I zoned out, letting my feet and my two of wands carry me towards the doorway to my secret passage. I thought of the trip with some satisfaction. I'd begun to bring a lantern with me—I could always manage enough of a temper to light a lantern after a day in the Magus's house—but I didn't think I would need it. Whatever backflip my brain or magic had needed to use fire without being angry, I thought I'd gotten it. For kicks, I conjured a small flame. It was only a tiny puff of fire, the same sort of thing Delia had been practicing with the ace of wands. It worked—flickering and dying quickly. Though I did not require it, rage would still let me draw on more power with ease. I'd need to practice pulling more power without the anger, but it was like I'd removed a spigot between me and the magic. It was just there—no emotion about it.

I crossed through another neighborhood, and then a third before I found myself surrounded by the familiar townhouses and deserted streets that told me I was close to my entrance to the Palace of Wands.

Which is when I—thankfully—caught sight of the Swords.

It was pure luck and no credit to me. I'd been increasingly careless about the walk between the Magus's house and home. I came around a corner as a man stuck his head out of an alley. The Sword had turned the wrong way, looking away from me first and then back towards me. I didn't recognize him, but he started when he saw my face and I froze. We locked eyes for a moment, and then he cursed and jumped out—three others following a moment later. They had swords.

I turned and sprinted away, picking an alley at random.

They were still behind me and I had a few seconds to think about whether I should go back towards the more crowded places I'd left or stick to this sleepy neighborhood. I might be able to lose them in a crowd. Or there might be more of them nearby. I reached for the fire. It was there.

I thought of the shadow monster I'd roasted. And of the Two of Swords dying.

The Two of Swords. Hector.

I turned toward the crowds. I ran past startled faces. People got out of my way—or they got out of the way of the Swords behind me.

I careened in front of a horse-drawn cart and plunged into another alley—it was cobbled and thankfully lead into a warren of twisty little streets that curved between buildings from every era. I picked directions at random and kept moving. I didn't look back.

I wasn't exactly in the best shape. Magic is hard work, but it's not a substitute for cardio. I was breathing hard and I didn't have any sense of whether I'd lost my pursuers.

I decided to pick a doorway and see if they were still following, just as I hit a dead end. The little street I was running on lead under an archway and ended in a courtyard with four or five stories towering around me. I dodged left around the archway, breathing hard—my breath fogging before me.

I put a hand to my deck. I didn't know what I was trying to find, but I hoped that my deck might have an idea. I pulled the ace of wands. Not subtle, but I thought it would help.

I heard running footsteps. They slowed as they got closer and almost stopped. I waited, away from where a sword might reach if they decided to stab around the corner.

I tried to catch my breath and watched the corner, hardly daring to blink. I held my magic at the ready. It wasn't a lot—I was worn out and not used to the new path I'd carved out for my magic, but it wasn't like I had much choice.

They didn't come around the corner.

I started wishing they bloody would, to get this over with.

They waited.

They were waiting for someone.

TWENTY-ONE

Tight Corner

CORNERED AND FEELING IRATE with the Swords, the City, and myself, I looked down at the ace in my hand. I'd never used it before, but that wasn't anything new.

Better to get it over with.

I pulled as much magic into me as I could stand. It wasn't a lot, comparatively. I was scared, not angry, and this was like stretching a new muscle. I'd need to be careful—or get angry. Cautiously, I edged around the courtyard wall as far as I dared—I definitely didn't want to let the guards near me with their weapons. Then I stepped out into the open, fire pouring from my hands and shooting forward.

I burned the air, then let it go as shouts erupted.

I hadn't hit anyone badly, but I certainly had their attention. They were sheltered on the other side of the gateway, backed against their own wall. Two had hands up, and gusts of wind redirected my fire—keeping them warm, but unburned. I felt them struggle to do even that—and I realized that my idea of strength was relative. These were guards, not Court Cards. I might be okay—if I got out of here before anyone else caught up with us.

I looked down the little cobbled street and saw no sign of whatever cavalry they were waiting for.

I took a deep breath, trying to steady myself.

"I'd really rather not fry you all," I shouted. My voice came out a touch high, but not too scared. I hoped.

They didn't respond.

I inched forward so I could see them better, still well out of a sword's reach. They were ready with spells of their own, but seemed nervous. None of them loosed any winds or other nonsense immediately.

"If you turn around and start walking now, I won't turn you all into charcoal," I said.

They glanced at each other. The one who was clearly in charge glanced back down the alley. Waiting.

"I'm not hanging out for whoever you're waiting on," I shouted, bracing myself to blast them. I didn't want to hurt anyone. Why didn't they just fucking turn around?

I was angry now, making it was easier to pull in more power. It was the strangest thing in the world—this morning I wouldn't have felt as bad about using fire to hurt these people. Because I wouldn't have been able to help it. Now I was furious, but I had more control. If I hurt them, it wouldn't be an accident. And I was going to do it. You should never make a threat you aren't willing to follow through on—especially in the City.

"Choose now," I said, my voice came out lower, sadder. It made me shiver. A second later I realized it was because I'd sounded like my mother.

They hesitated another moment. I thought I had them—they were nervous, for sure. The leader opened his mouth.

Right then we heard footsteps running towards us. I could have screamed in frustration. I saw their faces harden, their stances straighten.

So much for that...

I readied my ace to fight whoever was coming down the road and—

It was the Ten of Wands.

The consternation on the faces of the Swords lasted for half a heartbeat, and then the Ten sent lances of fire towards them. She struck two and they screamed. The guards stumbled and scrambled backwards into the court-yard, coming closer to me in order to get away from her. If I'd been of a more bloodthirsty temperament, I'm sure I could have killed them all.

"Charity, to me," the Ten snapped, her voice carrying without yelling.

I sent my own plume of fire towards the Swords—to make sure they backed off—and made a break for the archway. They let me go. I ran toward the Ten and she waved me behind her, not looking at me. I turned to see her send a second hail of fire lances into the wall and earth around where the Swords now cowered. They thudded down in bursts of flames, setting her in sharp silhouette.

She turned to me with her usual disapproving expression on her face.

"They were waiting for someone," I said.

"Then we should move," she said. "Come on."

TWENTY-TWO

Revelation

THE TEN OF WANDS DIDN'T RUN. She walked, purposefully, her back perfectly straight. People got out of her way faster than they had for me when I was going to literally run them over. I struggled to keep up without trotting, trying to walk like her and trying not to peer over my shoulder every other minute.

Her expression didn't exactly invite conversation. She didn't look at me, didn't once check to see if I was following or if we were being followed.

Within a few blocks, the people around us were predominantly Wands—turns out I'd been close to the palace.

She walked us straight to the gates of the Palace of Wands. The guards there were surprised to see her, but they snapped to attention and opened the small door hidden in the entwined metal of the gate for us.

Once inside, the Ten turned to me.

"What happened?" she demanded.

"I don't..." I said, annoyed that she wanted to do this now, here by the gate, "They were waiting, in the neighborhood where the passage lets out. I saw them before they saw me, so I ran. They followed, I got cornered. I nearly got out of that and then you showed up. What were you doing out there?"

Over her shoulder along one of the paths, I saw two people approaching: Delia and our Knight.

"They knew where to find you," said the Ten, "Have you seen any Swords before?"

"I haven't," I said, but, of course, I had. I'd thought about it while I was running and I've never felt quite so stupid in my life.

Hector had always known who I really was.

The first thing he saw me do was kill the shadow creature with fire. Sure, I could have been using the ace and I could have been a servant of the Magus, but he would have known that there was a Wand on the Fool's Path. He would have known I was recently accepted, and that the Magus's house was my next step. He might even have been told to watch out for me and he certainly would have been able to ask what I looked like. If I'd tricked him for a second, it had been blind luck—and even then he must have known for days who I was.

World damned twos. The twos of each suit embody a number of things, as the number itself does: balance, partnerships, and equality. They're also opposites and duplicity. I wondered if he'd told the Knight immediately, if they'd been watching me for days. It seemed unlikely— then they definitely would have caught me.

Delia ran the last couple yards between us while I hesitated on my answer. She came to stand defensively beside me, facing the Ten. The Knight stopped somewhere in the middle, indecisive.

"What's going on?" asked Delia.

"Miss Fool over here almost got herself killed by Swords."

"What?" the Knight was alarmed.

"I did not," I said.

"You were careless," said the Ten. True, but not why in the way she meant it. "You were careless, and you could have betrayed a palace secret. Or been hurt. Or captured or killed."

"I think they would have ambushed me closer to the door, if they knew exactly where it is," I said, subdued.

The Ten snorted, she looked at the Knight—who glanced away.

"I see," she said, but I thought it was in response to the Knight, not me. She considered Delia and then me. She pursed her lips.

"Do better," she snapped at me, and then turned away, her coat flaring. She marched off, no doubt to tell my mother what had happened.

"Do better," muttered Delia. "A great help, thanks for the wisdom..." She put an arm around me. "You okay, chérie?"

"Little shaky," I said. "But we've got some stuff to talk about. Not out here."

"Us too," said Delia, she tilted her head towards the Knight. "It's about the King."

The Knight looked resolute.

"Okay then," I said, and together we walked towards the palace.

TWENTY-THREE

Manipulation and Contingencies

WE RETURNED TO THE KNIGHT'S treehouse for our small conference. The palace had more opportunities for eaves-dropping, whereas the treehouse was made to the Knight's own specifications—and hopefully safer.

The Knight of Wands seemed embarrassed. He wasn't wearing the sling anymore and was back to his own neatly pressed self—his suit today was ember orange.

"Charity," he said. "I'm not sure where to start."

My heart sank. "Start with the King," I said.

"Have you... seen him?"

"When would I—" I stopped. The last time I'd seen the King of Wands had been when everyone had seen him. When the Queen had made her speech to the full House of Wands.

"He disappeared right after we all left the throne room. I haven't seen him since then," I said. "Why?"

He fiddled with his cuff.

"Sir... why?" I asked again, becoming alarmed.

Delia picked up the thread: "So, I was talking to the Seven, and he seemed to be worried, about the King being tired. And not very *present*. He seemed like... like he was sad because things were going back to the way they'd been before. I asked the Knight about it..." she prodded him in the knee, "Come on," she said.

"I didn't know him very well," explained the Knight. "Back then, before the Queen faked her death. I thought this was what he was like. Distant and forgetful."

"That doesn't sound like the King of Wands," I said, "At all."

"No, and he wasn't always like that—there were moments when he was..."

"Like when he stood up to her at the duel with the Princess of Wands," said Delia.

"Yes," said the Knight, nodding to her. "Those were odd moments though. He... I thought he stepped into his proper role because he had too, when the Queen was gone for awhile."

"She was doing something to him," I said, dread creeping in and then: "What is she doing?"

"I think she's using a seal," he said.

"A what?"

The Knight sighed, looking for a way to describe it simply. He said, "Most of the magic we do with cards is immediate, yes? There are other branches in cartomancy, and seals are one. They let us make stronger spells—building them through connecting several cards and leaving them in place—to create more complex and sustained effects. It's how... it's how she maintained the illusion of her death—and how she and the Ten kept up the illusion on her at your party. You asked if the Knight of Swords was especially strong. He is and his specialty is constructs. Our Queen is also that strong—but it's seals that she's particularly good at."

I tried to take that in. I've always been scared of her, but there's being scared and then there's realizing that I might still not be scared enough.

"The King," I asked. "Have you seen him?"

"He wouldn't see me today," said the Knight. "But I don't know—he might think I would help her. Be on her side."

I jumped to trying to think around the problem. Then I realized what he'd said. Silence lay between us, until I said: "You're not?"

The Knight closed his eyes, flinching.

"I missed her so much," he whispered, still with eyes closed. "When she was gone, Charity. I know it doesn't work this way, but I thought it might kill me. I thought we might all be done." He dragged in a shaky breath. "When she came back—I thought all I wanted was for her to be back. Except knowing—having something to compare the Court to... and the ways she..."

He opened his eyes and lifted his chin, determined. "There aren't sides," he said. "There shouldn't be, within the Court of Wands. Not the way she sees them. The way she sees them is the reason we have sides at all."

I nodded, surprisingly grateful and relieved to have him as an ally.

Delia let out an exasperated sigh and said, "You two don't know how to make up."

She levered herself up and threw her arms around the surprised Knight of Wands, hugging him tightly. He blinked, caught off guard, and held her awkwardly. He looked at me with some alarm over her shoulder.

Delia let him go. "Now," she said. "What's next?"

"Next is figuring out what she's doing or trying to do to the King," I said.

The Knight shook his head, flushed, and asked, "How are thing's going in the Magus's house?"

"What does that have to do with this?" I asked.

"Do you... if you're close to getting your focus, then we should wait while you get it," the Knight said. "I'm not strong enough to challenge the Queen of Wands directly. We could do it together, but if you had your focus, then we'd have a better chance. At everything—unraveling whatever spell she's holding on the King and not getting ensorcelled ourselves."

"You're worried that if you push, she'll try to enchant you too," I said.

The Knight of Wands nodded. "Right now, she thinks I'm hers. She's asked me to continue keeping an eye on Delia. In case you become a problem, Charity."

From Delia's total lack of surprise, I took it that he'd confessed that earlier. I shivered.

"I can handle pretending to be clueless," she said, with a hair flip. "And it means she's not suspicious of us spending time together."

I shook my head, trying to ignore the angry clamor in my stomach. "I don't know if I'm close," I said, "To getting my focus. I don't need to be angry to use fire now. My control is better."

"What?" said Delia. "Chérie! You did it!" It was my turn to get a fast flung hug. She squeezed me tight and I squeezed her back, laughing.

"Congratulations, Charity," said the Knight, also smiling. "Does anyone else know?"

I shook my head—I didn't think the Ten had been paying enough attention to notice.

"Good," said the Knight. "It's another surprise on our side... about your focus—"

"I'll try to get a better sense of it tomorrow," I promised. I hesitated, "You don't think she'll hurt the King? Permanently?"

The Knight shook his head, somewhat ashamed: "I think she was doing this for years," he said. "And he came out of it while she was pretending to be gone."

"I wonder why she stopped—while she was pretending to be dead," I said.

The Knight flinched. "I think the King knows what she's doing to him."

"Yikes," said Delia.

"So that's part of how she convinced him she'd died," I said, putting it together as I said it.

We all took a minute to think about how fucked up *that* was.

"How long does one usually stay in the Magus's house?" I asked.

"A month or more," said the Knight. "It's different for everyone."

I nodded. "I'll see what I can find out," I said. "But I don't want to wait a month. She might change her strategy—or realize she's not as strong anymore. She might realize you're behaving differently and come after you, and I don't want to risk the King."

"Agreed," said the Knight.

We left shortly after that, but before making our way out into the dark, I paused by the door with Delia.

"What is it?" asked the Knight.

I glanced at Delia.

"My mother is going to tell you to hurt Delia," I said. "At some point. She's going to realize what we're doing, and you're her ax over my head and hers. You know she'll try to use you."

The Knight nodded. I waited and he straightened up slightly.

"I'll defend her," he said, seriously. "I'll defend you."

"And we've got your back," I said. I offered him my hand and we shook with an odd formality.

Delia rolled her eyes, "You two... we already said that!"

TWENTY-FOUR

Keeping You Safe

BACK IN OUR ROOM, DELIA and I were both jumpy. Before going to bed Delia came to sit with me. Alphonso stalked between the rooms, yowling inquisitively at intervals.

Delia caught me up on her day—Seven was arranging for her to be taught the quarterstaff. Another skill I wished I could pick up.

I had trouble focusing on what Delia was saying, my brain spinning from one thought to another, starting with seals and the King.

What if the Queen tried placing a seal on me? On Delia?

How would we know? Could she just win outright? Without us putting up a fight at all—and what chance did we have if even the King couldn't break himself out? How *was* it possible for her to control the King so completely?

And then, there was Hector—and the Swords. What had he told his House? What would I be walking into when I went to the Magus's House tomorrow?

"We'll beat her," said Delia, apropos of nothing.

"What?"

"You're totally zoned out, kitten," she said. "You're worrying about your mother, right? And the King? We'll beat her. Once we figure out what's wrong with the King, it's going to be no contest."

"Yes," I said. "But also no." I sighed, not looking forward to this, but said, "We should actually talk about the Swords today."

"What? Was it really that close?"

"Not really," I said. "But it was my fault."

"What do you mean, kitten?" she asked.

"Do you remember the Two of Swords? She died at my party."

"Your mother zapped her," said Delia, distressed. "She died?"

"Yes," I said. I rushed to get the rest out, "And there's a new person training to be the Two. Part of their training is at the Magus's house. We ran into each other, and I lied about who I was, but I'm pretty sure that he knew who I was. I think that's how the Swords found me today."

Delia got very still while I said that. She kept her eyes firmly on the ground and asked, "When?"

"When did...?"

"When did you meet him in the Magus's house?"

I hesitated and then said, "It was the first day. I meant to tell you, but with everything else going on... it just slipped."

I wasn't sure what I was expecting from her next, but it wasn't what she said: "You can't go back."

"What?"

"To the Magus's house!" snapped Delia. Now she was glaring at me, "It's a trap now. There'll be Swords crawling all over the place, waiting for you!"

"I have to," I said, surprised. The Knight was correct about my focus helping our chances—and the more I learned about my mother's magic, the more help I thought we needed. All that aside, I was still stuck on the Fool's Path. I had to go back to the Magus's house.

"You do not!" she responded with heat. "The Fool shows up all over the place. Why do you have to be in this one specific house for the Magus, anyway?"

"It's the way the Path works," I said. "All the Major Arcana are different. This is how the Magus does things."

"Bullshit!" said Delia. "There's got to be another way."

Alphonso came to sit by the bed, he yowled in concern at the tone of Delia's voice.

"There isn't!" I snapped back.

Delia drew in an angry breath, nostrils flaring, "And why didn't you tell me? About the Two of Swords?"

"I meant to! I just did!" I'd gotten up, and was trying and failing to keep my cool. "In case you haven't noticed, there's a lot going on right now."

Delia's hands were clenched into little fists, "You're on me to be careful every fucking day," she said. "You basically told the Knight to take care of me *or else*. And you what? You've been buddy buddy with a Sword for a week? *And* you didn't tell anyone?"

She was crying. Delia hates to cry. She brushed the

tears away, angrily, with the side of one fist. She'd painted her a nails a cheerful dandelion yellow.

"Dee..." I said.

"They tried to kill you," she said. "They tried to murder you in front of me."

I didn't have anything to say to that.

"You can't go back right now," she said, pulling herself together and trying to take charge. "We'll tell the Knight. He'll understand. We'll just have to try to take on the Queen with less firepower. We could use you inside the palace for a few days anyway—to help get support here. You could talk to the Seven. Maybe we can get in to see the King."

My gut clenched. I remembered the Queen saying 'because I said so'. Delia didn't understand how dangerous my mother was.

"We'll lose."

"You don't know that."

"Yes, I do!" I said. I might have shouted. "She's going to be almost unstoppable even with the King and the Knight on our side! She's fucking powerful, Dee, and we need every inch of help we can get."

She glared at me.

"Then I'm coming with you," Delia said. "To the Magus's house."

"No! What the hell?"

"Why not?" She crossed her arms, her hair a halo around her face.

"Because you'd be in danger," I said, exasperated and irritated because she should understand this by now. "Dee, you're going to be a kick ass sorcerous. You're going to be better than me—it's easy to tell. You're getting actual training! From people who won't psychologically abuse you. Right now though, you'd be a fucking liability."

I regretted it as soon as I said it.

"I didn't mean that," I said.

Delia bit her lip, shaking a little. She got up.

"Dee..." I said again.

"Don't talk to me," Delia said. "I'm going to bed."

She walked into her room without another word.

Alphonso followed her, pausing only to give me his own wide-eyed *look* before disappearing—leaving me alone.

TWENTY-FIVE

Through the Door

THE NEXT MORNING I WOKE before the sun. I lay in bed briefly, but there was no way I was going to get back to sleep. I dressed and got ready for the day, telling myself it was because the early start would throw off the Swords—I'd been pretty consistent with the time I went to the Magus's house before now—and not because I was avoiding Delia.

She didn't move in the next room. I hesitated by our makeshift doorway—not sure if I should wake her, or if she was even awake already and waiting for me to leave. She'd told me not to talk to her.

Alphonso wandered in, swishing his tail, his eyes big and black in the low light.

I knelt down to scratch his ears.

"Tell her I'm sorry," I whispered. He didn't seem to approve of the sentiment any more than I knew Delia would. I felt queasy. Should I have let her come with me? Should I stay away from the Magus's house?

If she got hurt, it would be your fault.

If the King gets hurt, if the Knight gets hurt and I can't help them...

The queasiness got worse.

I left my room—my feet quiet on the carpets of empty hallways and down the broad abandoned staircases. I headed for the gate to the Palace of Wands. I'd decided I didn't want to take the secret passage—if I walked out the front gate it would be another chance to throw off the Swords by changing my routine. Hopefully the door to the Magus's house would be nearby.

The guards at the gate let me out. The street beyond had only a few people walking through the pre-dawn, and I took the wide boulevard straight away from the Palace, looking left and right for any sign of the Swords. I didn't see any of them. I had the Magus's card in my hand and set about finding the door.

It was hard to stay focused on the Magus. A dozen other thoughts intruded. I shook them off. Or tried to.

I could go back. I could apologize. Maybe Delia had been asleep and if I went back now, I could tell her I'd changed my mind.

I stopped in the street. I might have turned around then. Who knows what would have come out differently, if I had.

But the Magus's card in my hand twitched—the door was right there, nestled between a parfumerie and a haberdasher. World damn it all.

I entered to find the familiar long corridor with the coat

hooks—it was the only place that had remained consistent and stable during my time in the house. I hung my coat and then glanced at the others, wondering if one was Hector's.

He'd said he was done training with the Magus. I hoped that was true.

If we saw each other again, I might have to kill him.

Didn't want to think about whether I meant that literally or figuratively in my head.

I steeled myself for whatever the house was going to throw at me today, and went through the blue door.

I found myself in a small library, with dark wood walls and plush pink and green upholstered chairs.

The Magus sat in one of them, prim and younger than I'd seen him so far. His hair was only shoulder length, his face clean shaven and angular.

"Arcana," I said.

"Fool," he replied.

"I need to find my focus," I said, getting to the point immediately. "Or at least to know that I won't find it for awhile."

He seemed vaguely interested by that, and then—to my shock—he drew out a tarot deck and pulled a card. I'd never seen a Major Arcana with a deck—not that I'd had much chance to. He laid the card on a small table. It was Judgement—a Major Arcana. His version of the card depicted a figure on their knees, smiling under a bright sun—having just crawled out of their own grave. It made my skin crawl.

"Ordinarily," he said, looking at the card. "I prefer a longer apprenticeship—but it is not to be. The circumstances under which you walk the Fool's Path are strange, Charity Waits. Difficult. It's time for you to leave me soon. And much else, besides."

I allowed myself to hope, and then crushed the feeling. Things were never that simple in the City.

"I'm... not sure what you mean," I said. "Do I... I'm done? Training here?"

"Almost."

"So... where is my focus?"

"Where she left it," said the Magus.

He rose from his chair, leaving his deck and his card, and walked to one of the room's bookcases. He tugged on one of the books, and a shelf shifted, opening into a doorway.

There was nothing there, behind it. Not a dark passage, not a curtain. Just nothing.

The Magus gestured towards the doorway.

If I can get my focus and be back before lunch, maybe Delia won't be quite as mad at me.

I thought of the Fool then too, of their feet dangling over nothingness. I sent a quick sort of prayer to them, wherever they were, and stepped into the dark.

TWENTY-SIX

The Princess of Wands

I FOUND MYSELF IN A LARGE octagonal pavilion, carved stone under my feet and dark wood posts holding up the roof. Above me, the rafters of the pavilion were decorated in patterns of flowers and dragons. Surrounding the structure, coming right up to the edge of the stone floor was a lake. Stepping stones marked paths across the still water, one from each of the eight sides of the pavilion. It smelled like wood and the lake around us.

Beside me, one to either side, were the King and Knight of Wands. The King wore an oddly ornate costume—gold jewelry dripping from his neck and wrists and fingers. His enormous crown hid most of his curling black hair and the stiff collar of his overcoat was heavy with pearls and gold beads. The Knight, on the other hand, appeared much as he usually did—in a blood red suit, vest, and pants along with a pale yellow shirt and his golden wand cufflinks. His expression though was odd though. Excited. The Knight caught my eye, devotion raw in his face. I felt my lips curve in a small smile before I turned my eyes forward.

In front of us, walking away, was the Princess of Wands.

She wore a coat of leather sewn with ceramic discs, flashing in the dying sunlight. Her legs were protected with burnished grieves and metal plated boots. Her hair was short, and in one hand she held a ribbed, thin metal rod—her wand—roughly the length of a sword. Her steps were perfectly assured and she was flush with the power of the World—the final Major Arcana on the Fool's Path. She was beautiful.

The sun hovered above the horizon, sending rays of light directly into the pavilion, gilding her in golden light.

Walking towards my Princess from the other end of the pavilion was the Knight of Swords. He wore white and hadn't bothered with armor—his form was washed out in the glare of that bright sunlight. He seemed angelic in a twisted way.

I wanted to scream at her to stop. I knew what was going to happen.

But not all of me did. As I looked down, I saw a card in my hand. It was the Tower—the image depicting a literal tower, with lightning striking the top, and a single figure with pale hair falling from its height.

Aversion and fear hit me—why was I holding that card? I didn't have the right. I should *not* be holding the Tower. Why was I?

Then I knew.

I knew who I was. I knew whose skin I stood in.

I wasn't Charity. I was standing in my mother's skin. In this moment, I was the Queen of Wands as well as myself.

I knew that my Princess would win, because I was going to cheat to help her do so.

The Tower was full of energy in my hand. It wanted to be used—wanted to send someone plummeting unexpectedly down from the height of their power, wanted to tip things one way or the other. I knew how overconfident the Knight of Swords would be. I was sure I could use it to bend things *my way.*

I—I, Charity—was mortified, but the Queen of Wands was certain.

The Knight of Swords and the Princess of Wands stopped in front of each other.

"This is a bad idea," mumbled the King of Wands, beside me.

"Shut up," I said, casually. I had him on a short leash—my befuddled King.

"She's not experienced enough, not strong enough to take him," whined the King, persisting.

I gestured him to silence. I needed to focus.

"You could still concede," said the Princess of Wands.

The Knight didn't deign to answer. He had his sword out and in his hand. With his other, he drew a card and dropped it, saying: "I call on Justice to witness us here."

The Princess of Wands, all arrogant power, shrugged and forced a laugh. She drew a card from the deck on her hip and dropped it too.

"Sure, Justice as witness," she said.

I was so proud of her. I didn't know she was going to die.

Her card fluttered down to the stones, as the Knight's had. Then she readied her wand, her left hand prepared to draw another card.

Both courts held their breath, every eye on the Knight and the Princess...

...and then they gasped, because Justice appeared as the sun vanished.

Justice wore purple, a robe the color and texture of the night sky, and she stood perhaps eight feet tall. Her face was impassive, her eyes distant. She did not watch the fighters. She merely took a place, on one side of the pavilion, a living statue framed against the last gasp of pink and purple light in the sky.

Illumination flickered suddenly to life in the eyes and mouths of the wooden dragons in the rafters above us.

And I... I had the Tower in my hand. I couldn't use it now. Not with Justice actually here in attendance.

Major Arcana witnesses rarely *came* to duels—calling one was a formality. Why was Justice here? Why choose this duel, of all duels, to show up?

Not that it mattered, the Queen—I—told myself. She was good, my Princess, my Sabine. She could take him. She would. She had to.

The enemy Knight raised his sword in a salute and my Princess matched him casually, gracefully. She didn't care whether Justice or the World was there to witness. She was going to kill the Knight of Swords.

She could do this.

Sword and wand came together in a cascade of sparks. Winds whipped into dagger-sharp gusts and flames punched at the Knight. The Princess spun and harried him, showing off. The Knight fought coldly—never over-reaching on a single strike, only matching her as hard as he needed to. Some of her early attacks came close to him—singeing the white of his tunic, leaving burnt brown smudges on his sleeves.

This fight, this duel, was fought on three fronts though. The clashes of weapons and elemental magic were hard enough to follow—but both duelists were drawing and replacing cards from their tarot decks, looking for advantages, sending complex spells spinning between gouts of air and fire.

I, Charity, wanted to scream. Or to look away—but the Queen of Wands did neither. The Queen of Wands was confident.

The Knight started to pick up the pace, without losing any of his precision.

The Princess didn't notice at first. She used just as many flourishes in her blocks as she'd had for her strikes—dancing and meeting that sword and still spinning fire and cards with her other hand.

Didn't she see? Didn't she notice what was happening?

She did. I caught it in the set of her mouth as she backed, trying to find space that he was not giving her.

High and low, their weapons spun faster. She had the seven of wands in her hand, fighting off the Knight's magic with it. She wasn't switching cards anymore, all her attention on keeping up with the Knight.

She'd gotten used to the tight control of his strikes—he never pushed any more than he had to stop her blows.

When the Princess sliced her wand towards the Knight's

head and he caught it—she expected that same pressure. This time he pressed through—abruptly, brutally shoving her backwards. She stumbled, her wand thrown too far out of the way. She swung for the Knight, desperate to connect with something. She did, her weapon searing into his arm, burning him and sinking into the flesh while he ran her through.

He withdrew his sword smoothly, knocked her wand away, and caught her shoulder. The Knight spun the Princess around so that she was facing the Queen and her own court. I didn't want to see this—and I couldn't look away. His sword was at her throat already, and the Knight dug it hard into her neck—slitting a wide red smile under her chin. Her scream died in a wet wheeze and he dropped her.

The Court of Wands howled and wept and screamed. So did I. The Knight of Wands moved forward. I still had the Tower in my hand.

Fire. I needed fire.

I reached for it—screamed for it. Flames came rushing out of my hands and up, up into the pavilion. A wall of fire filled the space between the Court and the Swords. I threw all my weight, all my power behind it and the wall surged forward—then jolted to a halt.

At first I turned to Justice, to see why she would interfere. The duel was over. She wasn't a witness anymore, the damned Arcana.

Justice stood impassive, unseeing and uncaring.

It was the King, holding me back.

"Let go," I commanded him. He gritted his teeth, eyes averted from the wall of fire—my wall of fire—that he was pulling against.

"No," he said. I—the Queen of Wands—was surprised, shocked. Furious.

We fought for control of the wall of fire. He was strong. When had the King become so strong? I couldn't believe it—neither that the King was acting against me nor his timing.

Enraged and frustrated, I had to let it go. The fire rushed away from me, not so much as singeing the wretched Swords. I was left halfway between my court and the fallen form of my Princess. I almost attacked my King, punished him there and then. Instead I stepped forward to stand over my Sabine's body, facing the Knight of Swords—only a short space away, he looked to Justice, searching for some sign from her.

I wanted to pick up the Princess, but her head lay strangely, wrongly, held on only by the bone of her spine. I couldn't do it. I couldn't kneel down and take her in my arms. It was too much.

The Princess of Swords—almost as new as my Knight, a scant few years in her own post and not nearly as powerful as my Sabine—had come to stand by the Knight of Swords, to take his arm and pull him away.

"It was you I wanted," said the Knight of Swords to me. "She didn't have to die. I challenge you. Here and now. Let there be no more intermediaries between you and I."

"No," cried the King of Wands, come up behind us. "No more blood here today."

I hesitated. Then sneered.

"How about I fight her?" I said, pointing over the body of my own Princess to the Princess of Swords.

"No," said the Knight of Swords and the King of Wands together. "No more," said my King.

I had what I wanted though. I caught the panic in the Knight's eyes when I suggested fighting the Princess. I didn't know what she was to him—not like the last one— but I would find out. It would make my second Princess of Swords. Had anyone killed two before now?

The Tower was still in my hand.

"By the Tower, I'll be the one to kill you, Sir," I said, the words hot on my tongue. I pointed at his Princess, "But not before she's dead."

The courts gasped and I smiled. Let them do so. Let them try to predict me.

The Knight of Swords, already ghostly pale, turned whiter still and said: "By Justice, I'll see you dead first."

Once those words were out, everything froze. The ripples in the lake, the breathing of the two courts. It all was like a painting or a waxworks. Except for me—Charity.

I wasn't the Queen of Wands anymore. I was standing next to her frozen form.

TWENTY-SEVEN
Finding Focus

SICK AND HORRIFIED, I BACKPEDALED—finally apart from my mother's body and and back in my own. I stumbled and fell down.

The tableau in the pavilion around the Princess's body remained still and unmoving—my mother, the King of Wands, both Knights—all frozen like statues. I held tightly to the floor for a moment, shaking.

In the unnatural silence my own breathing was loud and ragged. I thought, for a moment, that that's all I could hear.

Then there were footsteps. The Magus was here too.

I stayed where I was and turned my head to see him. There was something frightening about this younger seeming Magus—all that power packed into too young a body.

He looked from me to my frozen mother.

"Interesting."

"What?" I snapped. I found I was rather remarkably pissed off at him. I wanted nothing to do with my mother, and being forced to *be* her... well. I was angry.

The Magus shook his head.

"What was the point of that?" I yelled from my knees.

He raised an eyebrow. "I believe you wanted your focus."

"Yes."

"Really, Charity, if you haven't found it here, I don't know what to do with you."

"I..."

I made myself look, with a sudden sinking feeling, towards the body of the last Princess of Wands.

My focus is where I left it. Where she left it.

I stood up and walked to Sabine's body, tense and sickened. The Princess's focus was still in her hand, the long gold rod she'd used to duel the Knight of Swords.

I bent down to take the focus from her hand and stopped. It didn't seem right, taking this from her body without... something.

I focused on her eyes and not the gaping wound in her neck.

"You shouldn't have died here," I said to her. I shuddered, belatedly feeling the kinship between the words and the thoughts of the Queen of Wands.

I picked up the focus that belongs to the Princess of Wands.

For a moment, it was just a piece of metal—then it warmed in my hand and changed. It shrank—rapidly going from half my height to a quarter and then smaller still. My focus shrank until it became about an inch tall, and when it was finished changing it hung from a fine gold chain. It was a necklace.

I put it on. My focus hummed to me—and of all things, my deck seemed pleased.

I stood up to face the Magus. He didn't say anything and I didn't know what I was supposed to say or do next.

He sighed, elegant, disappointed and unsurprised by my failings.

"You are..." he started.

"Unworthy?" I asked, still angry.

"Infuriating," he said. "I could do a lot with you, if we had the proper time. You may leave, now, Charity Waits." He waved a hand, and a wooden door appeared in the air.

"Thank you?" I hesitated. "Am I supposed to find the High Priestess then? I'm onto the next card on the Fool's Path? I passed the test or whatever?"

"Close enough," said the Magus, holding his forehead in one hand and waving me away with the other one. "Go on now. Shoo."

I stepped towards the door and then stopped again. "Thank you," I said, "For helping me use my magic without—"

"You really have the most unfortunate timing for developing civilities," the youthful Magus said. He turned and waved his hand a second time, creating a sort of mirror in the air or a window. It showed a street in the City—with the Knight of Swords running along it. He had a card out in his hand—the Magus—and hard on his heels were a half dozen of his guards. He was looking for the house. Horrified by the vision, I glanced back at the Magus.

"Really, Charity. What are you still doing here?"

I went for the he'd summoned door, finally.

It dumped me into the same study that I'd met the Magus in and, for a wonder, my blue door was still there as well. I kept moving and got out into the hallway. I grabbed my coat and went straight for the last door, the one that would get me out of the Magus's house—hopefully well before the Knight of Swords arrived.

I stepped into the street and ran into Hector.

TWENTY-EIGHT

In Which I Make A Mistake

HECTOR WAS AS SURPRISED as I was. We both backed up fast, putting our hands out towards each other. He wore two swords as silver earrings, dangling down on each side of his face and his coat was a dramatic white against his dark skin. We stood like that for a second, as still as those fucking memories in the Magus's house.

Then he started to slowly lower his hand, relaxing his stance.

The Ten of Wands came around a corner. She sent fire flying towards Hector without the slightest hesitation. He saw the flash and ducked, hurrying away from her.

It broke my trance and I ran towards the Ten. I grabbed her arm as I went, tugging her away from Hector and the Magus's house. She didn't move when I pulled even though she was smaller than me. She shouldn't have been able to do that.

"The Knight of Swords is coming," I said.

She nodded and turned back the way she'd come. I heard a whoosh of air as Hector summoned a construct, but we were already around the side of another building and away.

The Ten hurried me along. We ran through the City, dodging this way and that and coming quickly to the neighborhood that had the entrance to my secret passage.

"Why go back this way?" I asked. I supposed it might be closer.

"You went out the front gates," said the Ten, admonishing me.

"I thought it would be better than to risk giving away the other route," I said.

"You could have *asked*," said the Ten. "There's more than one bloody secret passage in and out of the Palace of Wands."

"Oh," I said.

"We're here now," she said. She slowed down, checking behind us and searching the roofs. Apparently satisfied, she opened the door for me with her own two and princess of wands. I went into the passage and lit the lamps nearby—feeling some unreasonable pride that I could do so with ease and without anger. The Ten closed the door and followed me as I took the lead down the passage. I was used to the skulls by now.

We moved in silence for a few steps, while I got my breathing under control. Then I said, "I didn't thank you for helping me the other day."

The Ten snorted.

"I'm trying to be nice," I said.

"Are you? Have you taken my advice to heart concerning the cohesion of the Court of Wands?"

I stayed quiet for a moment.

"I have," I said, somewhat against my better judgement.

She stopped and I found myself turning. I should keep my mouth shut, really. This wasn't the moment to try to turn the Ten of Wands. Was it?

"You have," she said. She didn't unbend in the slightest.

"Yes," I said.

"Your mother will be pleased to hear it."

"I doubt that," I said. I shouldn't have, but I did.

"Nevermind," I continued. "We should get back." I turned to go, but she didn't follow me.

"I am the Ten of Wands," she said.

"What does that have to do with anything?"

"It is my job," she said, explaining with plenty of condescension, "to carry the burdens of the Suit of Wands."

She drew out a card from her pocket and held it out to me, showing me the image. It was a ten of wands—not a living deck, but one she could use and leave behind. The figure on the card was an old woman, struggling to hold together a bundle of wands with a determined expression on her face. I took it from her.

"I am the Ten of Wands. Her Ten of Wands, but yours too."

"And the King's?" I quipped. "Do you carry his burdens or add to them?"

Something flickered across her face. "Ah," she said, "The King."

She knew. I would have bet my focus that she knew about my mother's seal on him.

Her gaze slid sideways, focusing on something behind me. I looked over my shoulder—the passage was empty. I turned back to the Ten and caught the end of her movement. Her wand, a short blunt club, thudded into my stomach. I fell backwards, all the air knocked out of me. I collapsed partially against the wall and got my hand up, summoning a fireball to fill the space.

The Ten stood in the center of it and was not burned. The flames licked around her, but I couldn't push them in to do any damage. I couldn't hold them for long either. The corner of her mouth twitched in a smile. She pulled two cards—one was the ace of wands and one was her own card again, the ten of wands from her living deck. With the ace, she spilled a tremendous amount of fire into the narrow hall—forcing me to scramble back. With the ten, she weighed me down. Every movement cost me, and I struggled to hold off the flames.

I still had her disposable ten in my hand. I held it up, channeling power through it—trying to hurt her with her own card, like a voodoo doll or something. Her card burned up in my hand. If I'd known what the hell I was doing, I think I could have beaten her with that. But I didn't know—and brute force wasn't enough. Her face twisted in pain and she dropped the two cards she'd been using to draw a new one: the four of swords. The figure on the card was either sleeping or dead. I wasn't sure which.

I drew another card, hoping for anything that might help. My deck gave me the queen of wands—and I had no idea what to do with that.

I tried to burn the card in the Ten's hand to ashes instead, but she was expecting that and she was stronger still. Her spell hit me.

My vision blurred. My arms grew heavy. I ground my teeth together and tried to keep my eyes open.

I felt her catch me as I slid sideways and then the world went dark.

TWENTY-NINE

Mother

WHEN I CAME TO, I DIDN'T know where I was. Then I saw the skulls. Then I remembered what had happened.

I turned my head and reached for my tarot deck in the same motion. My neck and stomach hurt like hell. My tarot deck was gone. I was shaky. This was not good.

"Hello, Charity," said my mother, standing somewhere nearby in the dim passage. She wore a stiff dress of gold and red with a wide lace collar. It stood out in points from her neck—like a deadly star. Her voice was different. Honest. *Fuck.*

"No," I said, not entirely sure what I was saying 'no' to. I struggled to stand, using the wall to prop myself up.

"You'll stay where you are," said the Queen of Wands.

"No," I mumbled, pushing myself further up the wall. The skulls seemed downright friendly, given the company.

146

"You will or the Ten will put you back under."

I drew in a shaky breath, finding the Ten where she stood in the shadows of the hallway. She had the four of swords in her hand still. It pressed down on me. My thoughts were muddled and slow. I slid back down the wall.

My mother crouched down, bringing herself close but not quite to my eye level.

"Now," she said. "What have you been saying to my Knight?"

"What?" I asked.

"My Knight."

"I haven't—" I started but she raised a hand.

"Let's not waste your time or mine, Charity."

I tried to conjure fire, but she shoved it down and away without twitching. I couldn't bring my mind into focus. My focus. I brought a hand up to my throat. She'd taken that too.

My mother saw the gesture and reached into her own pocket. She pulled out the necklace—my hard fought for fucking focus—and dangled it in front of my eyes.

"You were quick with this," she said. "A little too quick. The Magus went easy on you. I try not to take these things personally, but he doesn't like me. So it's hard not to."

"Maybe," I spat at her, "I'm just that good."

She snorted. "Oh, Charity. You're average. Raw power, yes, but no talent and no skill. No discipline."

I chuckled, weakly, looking away from her, "I always thought I would like it better if you were honest with me. Wrong again, I guess."

"We've wandered from the topic, *chérie*," she said and I flinched. "What have you been saying to my Knight?"

"Nothing," I said. "Not much. Though he's going to love to hear about this."

"Nothing?"

I tried to listen to the warning bells in my head—there was so much *wrong* with this situation that it was hard to find the right thread among all the knots.

We've got your back. I've got their backs. It wasn't about me. I was fucked. She needed to think I was the problem. Not them.

"I realized you were ensorcelling the King," I said, lying.

"How did you come to that conclusion?"

"Pieces here and there. A memory in the Magus's house. You're right. I don't think the Magus fucking likes you." The Magus could take care of himself against my mother. Delia and the Knight of Wands were in a more precarious position.

Her gaze drifted away from me, thinking about what I'd said.

"How did you know?" I asked.

"You think I can't tell when someone has fallen out of love with me?" she said, still not really paying attention to me. "The Knight is a terrible liar."

Finally she sighed and stood up, brushing invisible dust from her skirt.

"That's it?" I asked. "Can I get up now?"

She didn't answer.

"You need me," I said, searching for a way out. "There aren't enough Wands strong enough to walk the Fool's Path. You're stuck with me, if you want a chance against the Swords."

"No," she said, still looking into the distance, speaking as though to herself. "You may have brought the solution with you."

My stomach clenched, the adrenaline coming back with a vengeance.

Delia.

I wanted to cry. I wanted to tell her to leave Delia alone and knew that wouldn't help keep her safe.

"She's very good, your friend Delia. So the Knight tells me," said the Queen of Wands. "And she's much more... polite."

"More polite than I am," I whispered, trying not to choke on the words. "She's that strong?" It made me absurdly proud of her, even if it was going to help get me killed.

"With the right guidance," said my mother. "With a few years in the City. Perhaps." She smiled faintly, remembering, perhaps, her last protege.

I realized she was holding a card in her hand. I wondered if it was the Tower.

She returned her attention to me fully again, frowning, and said, "Do you know, you look so much like him?"

That took me a moment to follow and then I whispered, involuntarily, "My father?"

"It's been so long," she said, "I can't remember what he looked like—expect that he looked like you. Hard not to see him looking out at me from your eyes. He didn't think I'd kill him either, Charity. He thought he knew what I would do, who I was, and what I was capable of."

"You... you killed... you..." My father had been killed by Swords. I knew that.

How did I know that?

I reached for the fire again, but my mind clouded immediately as the Ten pushed me down. I almost fell unconscious. I let the magic go.

I thought back to my vision in the Magus's house.

Let them dare to predict me.

I didn't know what was happening. I felt sick and sleepy and I hated her. World damn it, I hated her, and no words or magic could express it. Something of it must have showed on my face though.

She watched me—distantly curious, and then she said, "I didn't want you back, Charity."

I blinked. I didn't understand.

"It's remarkable, the human capacity to make anything about themselves," she said.

"You... wanted me to be the Princess of Wands," I hissed, fighting to stay awake.

"No," she said. "I didn't. It never occurred to me that Swords would think of you. Or that Wands would follow."

That took another minute to sink in.

I thought of the last Princess of Wands, of the way it had felt to be on the edge of my mother's mind when she died. Sabine. My mother hadn't wanted me back. It was her Sabine she wanted—someone as ruthless and reckless as she was herself. If my mother hadn't found another Princess of Wands, it was as much because she was grieving for the last one as that she didn't like sharing power with people she didn't control. I was nowhere in that equation.

It had never been about her caring, about her loving me or hating me. I was certain, abruptly, that my mother had forgotten about me.

The Court of Swords remembered that she had a daughter, and thought I might be leverage or revenge or something—the King of Wands had remembered. She'd forgotten. Entirely.

It shouldn't have hurt at this point. She was a fucking murderer, and I'd hated her for years before knowing that, would have been delighted by the notion that she'd forgotten about me in the mundane world. Now, half lying against a cold wall, and increasingly certain that she meant to kill me—it wasn't that I wanted her to care, or that I gave a shit what she thought of me.

It just hurt bitterly that this was the mother I'd gotten.

"I admit," said the Queen of Wands, "That a part of me liked the idea when you appeared. It might have worked, if you were someone else. I hoped, briefly, but realized quickly that this wasn't going to work. Then you were moving too fast, becoming a threat too quickly—and you tried to take my Knight away."

What were they going to tell the Knight and Delia? I was crying and half-asleep.

I rolled my head towards the Ten. She still had that fucking four of swords in her hand. She was strong, the Ten, and it was a nasty spell. Fucking swords. Fucking Hector...

The two of swords.

I shifted, trying to push myself up. I heard my mother laugh without humor while I got a hand in my coat pocket. The card was there—Hector's card, a two of swords.

I'd used the two of disks to make a doorway, and the two of cups to find Delia—my better half. What could I do with the two of swords?

"So this is it?" I whispered.

"Yes," said my mother, raising a card. "You're dying better than he did. I suppose you are *my* daughter too."

Like all cards, the two of swords can be used in a dozen different ways. I needed to try something right now though and didn't have time to think it through.

I tried using the two of swords the way I had the two of disks—to make a door through which I could escape and be safe. I threw all my desperate last strength into it.

It did something. I just wasn't entirely sure what.

Epilogue

IT MIGHT HAVE BEEN A DREAM that I heard my mother scream as I disappeared, leaving her behind with an enormous burst of partially controlled magic. I don't think she would have screamed. She wasn't like that.

When I woke again, it was dark and I was very, very cold.

I risked summoning a small burst of fire without knowing where I was. It came hard, like the magic was moving through syrup.

The light burned my eyes, but I got a quick glimpse of what seemed like the same secret passage I'd been in. The hollow eyes of skulls looked back at me, but my mother and the Ten of Wands were both gone. And I was alive. So despite appearances, it seemed unlikely that that's where I was.

I still clutched what was left of Hector's two of swords

in my hand—only burnt fragments remained. I'd spent all its power to escape.

I held onto the ashy fragment as I stood, for no reason beyond I did not what to let it go. I limped along the corridor slowly—sliding my foot out in the dark and keeping my other hand on the wall of skulls.

My fingers found a gap and I risked another burst of fire. Passages broke off from the main corridor. I was in a different catacomb. I wondered which part of the City this was. I just needed to find a way out—and then find a way to warn Delia. Or the Knight.

I heard voices ahead, and couldn't tell what they were saying. I crouched down, uncertain if there was anywhere to hide and afraid to use fire without knowing who was there. Maybe I could follow whoever it was out of here. The voices stayed where they were and I crept forward.

As I edged closer I saw a flash ahead, and then the dim glow of steady light.

I came to a corner and found—to my shock—that the next walkway was lined with a plastic rope full of tiny electric lights.

I saw two people walk by wearing fashionable, but ordinary, clothes. Not robes, not couture, not medieval nonsense or embroidered jackets.

They saw me too, crouched in a dark doorway off the marked path with soot covering one hand, and definitely looking like a crazy person. They froze. Then one of them snapped a picture of me with their phone. They hurried away.

With their phone.

I closed my eyes and tried really, really hard not to panic.

It didn't work.

I was back in the mundane world, with no cards, no money, no passport and no way to get back to the City. Where my mother would be waiting, ready to kill me.

World damn it.

Thank You!

THANK YOU FOR READING **THE MAGUS'S HOUSE**!
If you enjoyed the story,
please take a moment to review it!

Check out www.arcananovels.com to stay up to date
with **Arcana** and join the newsletter for special extras—
including an exclusive story starring the Fool!

ARCANA
Charity's Story

The Fool's Path (May 2018)
The Magus's House (June 2018)
The High Priestess's Vigil (June 2018)

More coming soon!

AUTHOR'S NOTE
1. The Magus

IN TAROT, THE MAGUS OR THE MAGICIAN represents learning, mastery of magic, and power. He is often depicted standing alone over his tools, lord of all the elements and of spirit itself. The Magus—while he is still the beginning of the journey—also represents one of the Fool's potential conclusions: enlightenment made formidable by wisdom. The story that begins in the Fool card, may one day transform them into the Magus—but that's in the future. For now, we fools are here to learn.

You'll have noticed that in **Arcana** my Magus is a bit of curmudgeon. He's more a grumpy Merlin than a brilliant and mysterious Dumbledore. Most interpretations of the Magus are unalloyed and positive, but I tend to think of him as cold and arrogant too, and sometimes judgmental of those with other aspirations besides power through knowledge.

He's the Fool's mentor, but the Magus does not love the Fool. It's not that that Magus doesn't care—it's just that very few Fools are perfectly suited to the study and application which would make them a favorite of the Magus.

Part of what's fun, writing **Arcana**, is that the faces of the Major Arcana that Charity meets aren't necessarily the ones that, say, the King or the Knight of Wands met on their Path. Given Charity as his pupil, in this instance, I can't really blame the Magus for being a bit of a curmudgeon. Can you?

Acknowledgements

THIS IS INTERESTING, BECAUSE A lot of the same people who were instrumental in getting **The Fool's Path** down were also involved in **The Magus's House**. So I'm going to do something a little different. The Magus is a teacher, so I'm going to take the chance to thank some of my teachers.

Love to Mary, who read my very first short story—when it was ten pages longer than it was supposed to be.

Thanks to my very own 'good cop, bad cop' writing teacher duo: Banner and Kosmin. Every time I wrote a story, Kosmin asked: *why do I care?* Banner always told him to be nicer. Cheers, you two.

And dear Don-John... well, I can't think of a joke for this one. Thank you for being the sort of mentor you read about.

Thank you Aunt Joan for the lovely layout. Thank you

Silver and Kaija for the gorgeous covers and the pep talks and the everything.

Once again, Damian kept my sanity together through this project.

And finally, thanks to everyone who read the book. Seriously. You're the reason the work is worth it.

CPSIA information can be obtained
at www.ICGtesting.com
Printed in the USA
FFHW022101280619
53255409-58952FF